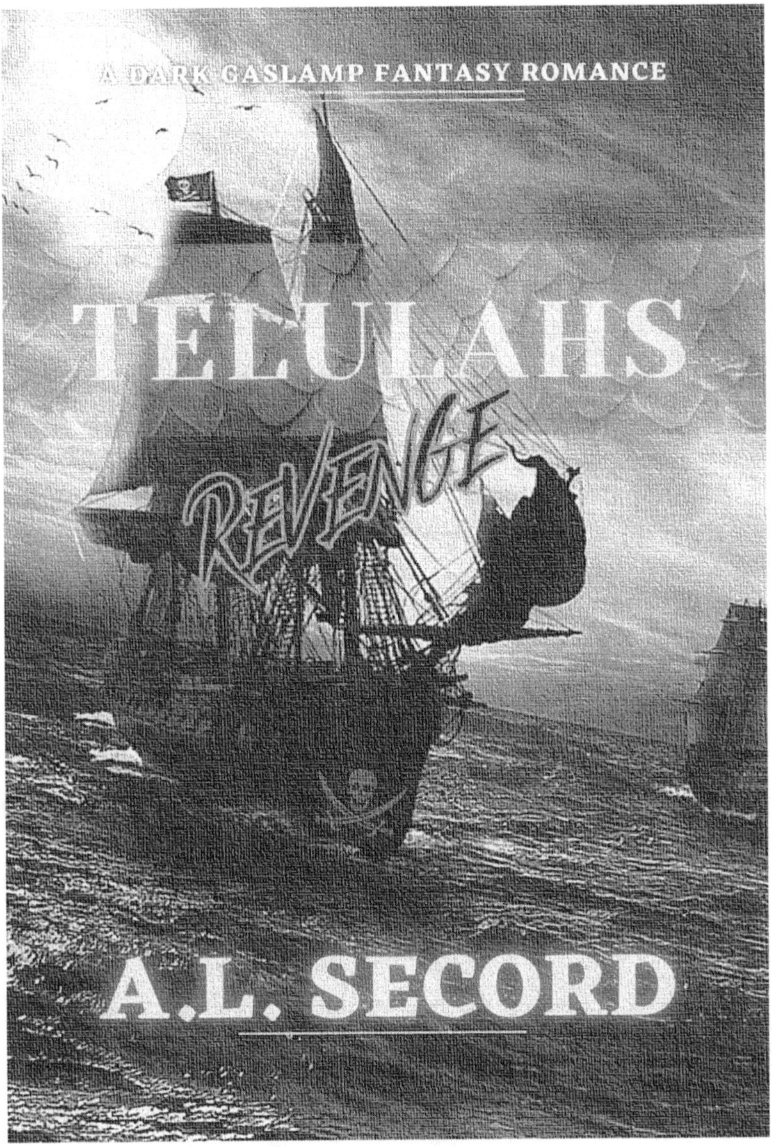
A DARK GASLAMP FANTASY ROMANCE
TELULAHS
REVENGE
A.L. SECORD

TELULAHS REVENGE

A DARK GASLAMP FANTASY ROMANCE

Written by: A.L. SECORD

DARK FANTASY WEREWOLF MAGIC PUBLISHING

CHAPTER 1

As I practiced my swordsmanship on the new recruit, I smiled wickedly at his mistake. He had gone left for the kill as I ducked to the right and stabbed his exposed right abs with my wooden practice sword. My crewmate and adversary was not impressed with his misfortune. Shortblade's beautiful golden locks flipped as his angry blue eyes looked at me in distaste.

"A mere cabin boy bested me? The sun was obviously in my eyes." Shortblade's voice was deep and snide as he glared at me.

"Has the sun been in your eyes the last six times the Lad has bested you Shortblade? I think you don't want to admit the Lad is good. He was trained by the best of course." I smiled as First mate Hatley cleared his jolly throat in taking credit even though everyone on our ship knew the Pirate King had trained me.

The Pirate King hadn't been easy on me either. I used to go to bed bloody and bruised for months until I was quicker in learning his mannerisms. I had to learn or it was the deep blue locker for me. I had to win my right to be worthy of being a crewmate and part of the Pirate King's clan. *That was almost seven years ago. What a time of adventure and freedom it has been since.* I thought for a moment as everyone stopped what they were doing and toed the line without the Captain giving the order.

To the entire world our Captain was the great leader of all the pirates. He was royalty and exalted. He was our great King. But he was also known by another name to the lesser civilized people. They called him; *'The Sun Dancer King.'*

It was a name given from the Evil King Vermin of Bristol in his mocked fury. Evil King Vermin's golden treasure was ravaged by a creature of the night that had also seduced his Queen in equal vengefulness during the day. And even though the Evil King Vermin of Bristol had given the order to behead his wife; our beloved *'Sun Dancer King'* had been blamed for her death. This didn't matter to us pirates. We would blindly follow him anywhere. We are his crew and we are the pirates that port towns feared and ladies swooned over.

Our ship unusually swayed in the calm blue waters and the breeze blew through my many layers of linen as I faced forward smiling with the other smiling crew.

"Good job Dragonfly. Shortblade you can learn from our young friend here. He has had to work ten times harder than that of any of the crew just to be worthy in my presence. He be' a dreaming land lover and not able to swab the deck before." Our great Captain's voice was a deep scruff like he always had to clear his throat.

The Captain chuckled warmly and we all laughed with him. But he was right; I couldn't swab the deck to save my life back then. The Captain's voice always seemed menacing and as fierce as the harshest hurricane; even in laughter. But he was our grand blue eyed Captain of our lovely; *'Telulahs Revenge.'* Tis' the fastest ship in all the sea and with the most fearsome crew. I loved our reputation for being merciless and I loved being a part of this misfit bunch of bandits.

I think we had always been family but we really bonded a couple of weeks back when the Royal Guard captured us and branded our forearms with the mark of the pirate. It was our first time being captured. There was truth about this scary bunch of men whom I called my blood brothers. We all abided by the code. And not one took treasure from the other or ever held a thought of mutiny. We had been through too much over the years and the Pirate King was too supernatural to double cross and live.

To be a new recruit on Telulahs Revenge was a big deal. You had to earn a place and pass a bravery test. Shortblade was a new recruit and had won the right to sail with us. He had his sea legs but he was too beautiful to be a pirate. I looked over at his handsome features and frilly shirts and smirked. *I bested you Dandy, six out of six. Take that you defamed nobleman.* I thought as I looked over to his muscular chest glistening in the sun. Shortblade always had the nicest of linen and high quality lace around his shimmering golden locks. I guess I was jealous. Actually I knew I was envious of his beautiful blonde hair and I hated my very feminine features and short, curly red hair under my black bandana.

Of course what did I know, I was only the cabin boy? I was the Pirate King's personal assistant-slave, but I loved every minute of it. I enjoyed being around such an amazing human. I wanted to be the best pirate ever, all because of his conquests.

The *'Isle of Fleshed Carnage'* is our spooky home sweet home, away from Telulahs Revenge. We dock there at least once a month when possible. Tis' always around full moons. There are many theories about that, but none of them matter to me. I don't focus on gossip. I absolutely love our haunted island of our home. The island is full of magic and hidden secrets. This is ironic since I have a rather big, hidden secret. I guess I blend in with the creatures and ghost stories.

The Isle of Fleshed Carnage was also home to man-eating mermaids called sirens; and a horrific hell hound blessed by Hades himself. It was rumored the werewolf could transform to something even more gruesome, but I had only met the beast once and that was enough for my fair heart. The beast had a terrifying howl that could make your ears bleed if you listened too long. Its horrendous sight could cause a man's heart to stop. The creature ate anyone and anything in its presence except for the pirates that had passed the bravery test. I thought about all this as the Captain explained about us docking for a bit, to gather and plot our next destinations. His deep voice sounded soothing as I let my mind drift.

I then looked with glee upon the castle that could barely be seen through the forest tree line of the island.

"Dragonfly where were you just now?" His voice was deep and magmatic.

"I...uh. I'm here for you Captain." I said and stuck my chest out and tried to look more serious.

"Yes my pirate daydreamer. Fetch a tea for me. I will be below. Hatley take the helm. Everyone dismissed." His scary stern voice held restlessness in waking me from my daydreams.

"Ahoy Captain." We all said in unison and then dispersed.

The Captain had been resting a lot since our capture and rescue. He was refined and cultured with only the finest of everything but that was how we were caught with a trading company commissioned by the Evil King Vermin of Bristol.

He seemed more tired and edgy like he was going to eat someone if they blinked twice in his direction. Although he wouldn't ever harm us, unless any of us crossed him. But that would never happen. Other than loving him, we all were terrified in suspecting he was full of dark magic and not completely human.

I scurried to the galley not before being tripped by Shortblade and then he winked. I frowned but got up quickly. The Captain needed me and that was the only thing that mattered. My smile was wide as I prepared the Captain's cup out of pure admiration. Then I rushed below deck and knocked on his door gingerly.

"Come in Dragonfly. I appreciate the curtesy knock but let it be reserved for when I have intimate company. We are all men here and I am waiting for you. I am so exhausted. Get my boots for me." His voice was deep and intimidating.

"Yes Captain." I replied and tried not to sound too happy about helping him, but I knew he knew.

My eyes had stars for the Captain since he first saved me and even though his presence was intimidating; I couldn't stop the loving glances I gave him. I was positive he assumed it was puppy love as he had nicknamed me; *Pet*.

I passed him carefully the mug as he looked out his chamber window towards the island on the horizon. He sat on his bed and lifted each foot so I could discard his heavy buckled boots. Then he moved to his winged back chair so I could give him a foot message. I loved really rubbing and working out the knots in his feet. Sometimes he would tell me great stories as I gently kneaded the pads of his tired feet. But today he sat with his eyes closed as I looked at his strong facial features and trimmed beard. His chin was square and larger which showed strength in itself and I couldn't stop myself from gazing upon his full red lips forbiddenly.

For some reason this last year I had to really check my feelings. I went from admiring him like all the men did; to something else new entirely to me. It was silly of me. I had just turned twenty and should have more adult feelings of adventure. But it was like a switch had turned on in me the past year that I couldn't turn off. And If I was more honest in thinking; my feelings had probably been growing towards him for the last few years.

My heart started racing when his blue eyes opened into my soul. It was like my heart wanted more which was quite impossible. Other than having no rank on the ship; to confess my feelings would mean the gallows for me. I quickly looked down to his lovely feet and rubbed a little harder. I could never say out loud how much I desired him because that would mean giving up my family and life as I knew it. The cabin boy was the part I played since I was thirteen but as I turned twenty; it was getting harder and harder to wrap my continually blossoming bosom. I wore extra clothes to conceal my certain qualities that none of the other men had.

I was born unfortunately, a girl. And in this man's world in 1717, I was a hidden unwed spinster of a criminal. It hurt to deceive them, especially someone I loved very deeply. We were all criminals to a certain extent but I didn't think they would let me live otherwise.

"Dragonfly I need help sleeping. I want you to sing to me that lullaby you know while messaging me and I will try to rest. Use that lavender oil we acquired from France it soothes me." His dark voice eerily said.

"Yes Captain." I said as I went to his personal cabinet and heard him rustling about while I got the giant bottle.

I turned around and knew my cheeks had gone rosy as he discarded his coat, vest and shirt slowly in front of me. He had this look of trust in his eyes and my guilty heart tried to stop desiring him. His fierce blue eyes never left mine and I turned away as he unbuckled his belt.

"Captain, I hear that Hatley gives a grand back massage." I said and hoped he had covered up his handsome tanned skin.

"No. His hands are rough and large. Yours are firm but gentle in touch and much softer. You have the delicate hands of any fine key master. I want you to do it. Hatley is like the mother hen of us all but you are my fine thief with delicate hands." His voice sounded sultry to me.

"Yes, my King." I said as I turned back and noticed he hadn't moved a muscle and frowned at this predicament.

He sat there upright with his belt off and his dewdrop skin glistened as the sun streamed over his powerful chest. Every inch of him was muscular and he was much leaner as I looked at his rippling abs. I waited for orders as my eyes tried to stay on his. He rolled his stunning blue eyes and then looked cross as I stood there.

"Dragonfly, I can't sleep with the curtains open." His deep voice said impatiently as he stood up studying me.

"Oh yes, you are correct my King." I said blushing and almost tripped across the room to close the three curtains.

The weight of his glance at me through the slightly darkened room was heavy but I refused to be devious. He had sheltered me and given me protection. And I would do whatever it takes not to vilify myself with peaking at his endowed gloriousness which I had breathtakingly seen many times before. But just as that moment of thought escaped my mind; I turned back to him and he slowly discarded his pants. He had completely stretched and yawned as he smoothed his long black hair. I immediately covered my eyes but it was too late and I had seen once again the splendor of every inch of his beauty, even with the sun beaming behind the light curtains. The sun was too big and too bright; and it was getting too hot in this room suddenly.

"Dragonfly, place my pants over the chair and uncover your eyes. I don't want you spilling your blood trying to give me privacy." His deep voice was stern but softer.

"Yes Captain." I said and gulped quietly.

The menacing Pirate King had turned over on his stomach. His firm glutes stood out and made me exhale in a heavy sigh. But then I gasped at the long gashes across his back. Slowly, I picked up his pants as he turned his head to watch me fold them and place them neatly on the chair. I stopped beside the stand and went back to pour a little lavender oil on my hands. *I love this scent.* I thought as my shaking hands touched his strong shoulders.

"Start at my shoulders and don't stop." He whispered in his scruff of a voice that almost sounded like the purr of a kitten as I started tenderly getting knots out of his shoulders.

"Why are you trembling at my touch today? You have given me many massages. Are you ill, my Pet?" His deep voice held concern as I tried not to shake.

"No I am fine, my King. Must have been not enough rum at lunch." I whispered back but his lovely bare skin felt like lightning and it zapped me in my loving caress of his shoulders.

Then there were these deep gashes that were angry hateful, red-lines across his back and far too many to count. As I slowly rubbed the raised skin I heard him hold his breath. His whole body suddenly twitched and straightened.

"I'm sorry Captain. I would never hurt you." I said and tried to work the butchered wounds again.

With one swift action, quicker than I could blink, he sat up and grabbed both my hands. His chest heaved quite heavily and I gasped as his eyes changed red and back to blue. His body was shaking in agony and had broken out in a sweat. I trembled at how close we were in this situation. I believe it was too close, as his hands held mine tight. Not to hurt me but holding onto something to stop the pain; as I had done to him lots of times before.

"I know you won't hurt me. I just think I need to heal more. The Royal Guards used silver this time and we were lucky to escape. Just my lower back and legs Dragonfly." He whispered out of breath and I could see true anguish in his eyes which he had never ever shown before.

As he let go of my hands it broke my heart, in seeing him carefully lay down on his stomach again. Suddenly my feelings were reinforced by his soft vulnerability. I knew who my alliance would always be with. No one in this world could ever force or bribe me to hurt this man. My whole soul flew to him in holding his spirit as I had just hurt him. I tried not to cry and held my breath as I worked on the knots in his lower back avoiding the ends of the lines. His skin was clammy now, but still felt like captured lightning every time I caressed him.

Singing softly, I sang my pirate lullaby and could hear him slightly humming with me as a deep contented sleep overtook him.

His hypnotic snoring was making me less than steadfast as I carefully took a sheet out of the closet and covered him. I knew we were close to the island but wondered if we would make it before nightfall with the stale winds at this hour.

❧❧❧

CHAPTER 2

I knew he was carrying me as I smelt the lavender and his natural sea moss scent off his skin. I'm not sure when he had awoke and when I had fallen asleep but I knew as I half-dreamt that I was in his arms. And I hugged him forbiddenly. His skin to touch was hot and its dew was across the rippling abs I had dragged and clutched my fingers to. I felt this shocking sensation on his skin softly zapping my fingers as I moved my hand over to his heart.

Everyone feared the great King of all the pirates and I did too. But we also loved our Captain. I knew it was good to keep distance though. The rumors I didn't listen to about the Captain were horrifying in nature. But still I dreamt of him. When he placed me in my bed and covered me under my chin; I reached up and held his hand. His head was by mine as I felt his breath on my cheek, when I kissed his rough hand. In this ultimate forbidden romance of a whimsical dream; I felt fearless and pulled his face to mine. He froze as my lips found his. Then he started completely kissing me back with the taste of brandy heavy in his mouth. I whispered in-between sucking on his earlobe in sugary kisses; *"I love you my King."*

I heard a soft growl as he gave me even sweeter kisses back and then I drifted off into lovely bliss of sleep.

🌾🌾🌾🌾

I awoke in the early morning hours in my small room in the castle. What a fantastical dream I had with the Captain. He always found me and carried me to my room. But this was the first time I dreamt of daring to kiss him. Such a tender vision I wish I could go back to, but I have chores. My heart raced at my endearing dream and I stretched and yawned softly.

The sun was not quite up yet and I could hear the prettiest songbirds outside my window. *What a wonderful day it will be.* I stretched once more and frowned as I looked down at the layers of cotton concealing my secret pounds of flesh. *I will have to wrap tighter and add more layers of fabric.* I thought as I looked down and frowned at the budding sight and fixed my loose wrapping under my shirt.

Completely ignoring my dismay I stretched again and looked out my castle window to the gardens of the courtyard completely excited to be home again. This was the place where we could all be free.

The whole island was owned by the Pirate King and no one dared to come here without an invitation because of the beast. I knew our King had some kind of power over the creature of darkness that roamed freely through the night. But since my bravery test, I had not seen the creature of darkness. *Thank goodness too.* I thought back to that night with the beast's long snout against my then flat chest breathing me in as I was cornered against the cliff wall and shuddered.

I ran down the few steps to the castle kitchen and got a nice fire going. Boiling the water for the Captain's morning coffee beaned brew and added a stick of honeycomb to the mug. Stepping outside the kitchen door; I accidently pricked myself on the thorns of the rose I picked for my King. He secretly loved roses and I plucked him a plump rose each morning. Most mornings I wasn't as clumsy though and I hoped the blood would stop leaking out of my finger.

Ignoring my bloody finger, I made my way past my door and further up the stairs of the castle tower to the Captain's bedroom. Our bedrooms were the only ones off the galley kitchen and in the tower. I loved the privacy of my own room and being so close to the Captain.

I slowly opened his creaky door and set his mug down on his little table beside his bed just like every morning we were at the castle. But I gasped at seeing his bed empty. Very rarely did this happen, but every now and then the Captain would sleepwalk. I found him a couple of times before the sun and men arose and would sneak him back into the sleeping castle. It was always our secret and I loved in keeping it for him.

I hurried out of the castle and past the plank foot bridge into the deep forest. I then gasped at seeing him in the meadow covered in blood and parts of rabbit viscera. He was sleeping soundly and the blood covered most of his dewdrop skin. I went over to him and shook him whispering softly for him to wake. When he rolled over to see me he looked confused as he grabbed his head. His whole face was red with the rabbit's blood and the pale blue of his eyes were eerie as they stood out like starlings through the carnage and gore.

"Dragonfly, why am I in the meadow and naked?" His voice was deep and downhearted.

"Tis' okay sir, you just had a bad dream tis' all. Come with me and we can get you cleaned up." I softly said as I unbuttoned my long coat.

"Yes, let us be gone from here." His voice seemed weaker than before as I took off my oversized coat and covered him.

He leaned on me as we travelled barefoot to the waterfalls and walked into the freezing water together. We paused only to discard my long coat on the shore. He went slowly to the waterfall and stood in its blue waters. And I watched him at first in good intentions. I wanted to be there in case he slipped or fell. We stood in semi-deep water and I was to be damned if I was going to let my King drown.

But as his eyes closed and the water cascaded down his handsome bloody face and red powerful body; my breath escaped me. I was close enough to reach him if he fell. But too close to the situation as it seemed he was having some intimate time cleaning. He stood there with his biceps flexed and his hands smoothing his long black hair down to his robust bottom and then slowly turned around in the waterfall facing me.

I knew my breathing had changed heavily. I couldn't help but stare at the water trickling down the curves of his body stretching and his large hands were frantically rubbing away blood. His eyes stayed closed as his arms flexed resting on his head. The actual water level sat below his strong hips. His navel was fully exposed and capturing the now pinkish water turning clear. Just underneath was a secret treasure trove of dark hair leading somewhere below the water's surface and with each of his slow purposeful movements his very bulky legacy would be apparent.

My eyes went wide and my heart was un-naturally fast again as I knew it was time to turn from this torment of my torn soul. But I feverishly indulged as I watched him raise each potent thigh to the flow. Those thick muscles connected to his equally sturdy knee caps and I loved the tenderness of his rough hands that seemed to slide everywhere and in-between. He was simply the most stunning person I had ever met. Even with the disturbing chaos I had found him in; he seemed like an angel. He was not meant for mere mortal eyes and I turned around quickly as my heart beat too fast for him. *Why is my heart betraying our friendship? Why do I have to be so attracted to my King? What is the matter with me? I have never felt such strong feelings before and it kills me to think so indecent. He saved my life and I need to stop fantasizing over him.* I thought as I submerged myself and tried to drown my thoughts in the frigid water.

I felt his strong hands lifting me. And when I broke the water's surface I inhaled deeply the oxygen my lungs desperately needed; but my eyes stayed close.

"Dragonfly, what am I going to do with you?" His deep voice sounded out of breath.

"Keep me because I make a good coffee my Liege." I said trying to be cheerful in this vigorous situation.

He let me go as he helped me up and I ran back out of the water grabbing my coat as I seen him shivering. I turned my head as he came out of the water and held the coat up for him. I was used to being outside and cold but being around him gave me the warmth I needed in waiting for the sun to fully rise. The morning had been chilly but I was not concerned as I fully buttoned the coat for him. I was soaked but I didn't mind. The tropical heat would have me dry before the sun was high.

"Dragonfly, this has to be our secret. I do not wish to perpetrate worry into the men's hearts. I am asking this of you as your King; and as your closest of friends these nearly seven years. I implore your absoluteness in this matter." I could hear the depleting power in his deep voice that whispered straight into my soul.

"Of course, my eminence and dearest of friends; you can count on me. You have my undying loyalty until eternity." I said softly as I helped him over the rocks and he leaned on me.

My arm was around the buttoned coat of his waist supporting his tall, bulky frame and he had his arm around my shoulder heavy as it rested. The dawn's light was all around us but the sun had yet to show, as pinks streaked across the sky.

"I need a moment Dragonfly. Let us sit under that tree a spell." His deep voice was out-of-breath and worrisome.

"Yes your Greatness." I whispered and frowned.

"I give you permission to call me Dragon in only each other's companies. It is my royal birth name. I was born Prince Dragon Wolfheart III, in a kingdom, oceans from here. It was a marvelous place. The palace had never ending supplies of loving fulfilling women, and ever flowing wine." His deep voice sounded wounded as he sat there with a whimsical smile in remembrance.

When he had sat against the tree his strong beefy legs stretched out of the coat. I held my breath as the blush spread across my face. His sharp blue eyes went straight to my bashfulness and I turned from his gaze. I knew he had caught my betraying green eyes travelling to his mammoth that lay scarcely hidden underneath the partially opened coat. My breath escaped me and I walked slowly away from where he sat. I stilled my wild thoughts and looked at the peacefulness of the magnificent sky. When I turned back he was slumped to the grass.

"My King…My King. Please Dragon, please wake." I said frantically as I moved his heavy body up against the tree and let my tears silently fall as I placed my hands on each side of his face.

I placed my head over his heart to hear the rapid weak beating and looked up again into his tired face. His penetrating blue eyes looked into my panicky green eyes.

"Dragonfly, I need your help. I need something from you. I wasn't able to get after we were captured and up until now. I need it or I shall perish into dust. I can feel it my bones. The rabbits were not enough." His soft blue eyes were as soft as his strained voice.

"Yes, I will give anything for your life my King." I said still shocked at his weakened state.

"Close your eyes now and trust that I will not harm you. I give you my word. I will have the magic to heal myself and your neck after." His deep voice seemed even weaker.

"Yes, I lay myself in willing sacrifice at your merciful feet. I would gladly give anything to keep you from dying my King." I said as my tears kept rolling down my cheek and closed my eyes.

I suddenly felt his hand gently moving my tears away in a sweet caress. His body shifted as he cradled my upper body in his arms. I could feel him unbutton the top buttons of my shirt and then try to move me closer. He froze suddenly as his hands tried to grab onto my side to lift me closer and instead grabbed both handfuls of my carefully concealed secrets. I heard his gasp in sync with my own and prayed he ignored what his hands were still holding. Gently he let them go, moving his hands to my back pulling me even closer.

His soft lips were suddenly on my neck and I felt his dry tongue, leathery kissing the spot above my now exposed clavicle. A deep growl came from his throat and then I felt his fanged teeth pierce my sun-kissed skin. The feeling went from pain to euphoria. His hot breath was on my neck as my heart fluttered wildly and felt his now moist tongue in a kiss. He kissed me sweetly once more and then placed my head against his madly beating heart. I could feel his chest inhaling and exhaling out of breath. And I could feel his whole body surging with stamina and zest.

"Oh my dearest of Dragonflies; in your fair blood I can feel the healing love in your heart for me. And your blood confirms the stolen glances your exquisite green eyes hide." He softly whispered as I lay in his arms tired but extremely happy with my eyes tightly closed.

"You have nothing to fear my sweet Poesia." He softly whispered the name of which I was born and hadn't heard in a very long time as I sighed.

His strong arms lifted me up gently and I felt like we were flying but I was so tired, my eye lids stayed shut. I could feel the weight of his stare though, studying me as I held him tight.

CHAPTER 3

I awoke with the mid-sun through my window and gasped. *What a strange dream I had. I really need to stop these odd feelings for the Captain.* I thought and looked at my drenched clothes and my heart beat wild as my brain panicked.

I repeated the steps that I did daily but floated in-between the other men doing their daily chores. The water was already boiling as Hatley had made an incredible breakfast which I inhaled as the other men ate. A little plate was saved for me by the stove which I decided to bring to the Captain instead. I went outside briefly and plucked a rose pricking the same finger from before as it dripped and I ignored it gathering the Captain's mug and plate.

I made my way up the tower steps carefully opening the door and my mouth dropped open to see the Captain sitting in his winged back chair. His beautiful bare chest exposed and bare legs with my coat adorned over him like a blanket. His peaceful snoring was in tune with the bluebirds at his window.

Quietly I placed the mug, plate and rose beside the other mug. My eyes went wide as I stood up removing the mug and his eyes were now open. His eerie blue gaze looked more charming and magmatic than ever. He grabbed my injured finger gently and I stood spellbound by the passion of his stare. His lips went to the blood that was still rushing out of the cut from the thorn. Slowly he kissed my finger and sucked on it as I held my breath in sweet ecstasy. He cocked his beautiful head back and his brilliant blue eyes closed as his fangs had elongated in a devilish smile.

I stood there breathless in knowing his truth. Once his captivating red eyes opened I couldn't look away as he secretly stole my heart. He still held my hand and brought it to his lovely lips once more sucking on the blood. He kissed it passionately as his eyes glowed in some kind of fairy magic.

My heart was beating so fast I felt like it was going to come out of my chest as I wanted his lips to taste mine but stood frozen in his God-like presence. He still held my hand and kissed it while I was lost in the depths of his starry blue eyes.

I knelt in front of him as I leaned into my coat across his lap so he could drink more and I was filled with an indescribable bliss as he drank from my finger. I didn't say a word as I closed my eyes. His other large hand caressed my face with his thumb stopping on my lips. Sweetly he touched my wanting lips as I held my breath and very slowly I removed my hat. *I am ready Dragon.* I thought as I could smell the heavy brandy off his lips and I brought my hand forbiddenly to his cheek.

I opened my eyes in uncontrollable adoration needing to touch his face. His red eyes were intensely watching me as he drank from my finger and I sweetly moved his long black hair behind his ear. As I did so I swept my fingers down his shoulder to his flexed arm and across his chest to his heart. His posture straightened as he closed his eyes and let my hand caress his skin in loving tingling touches sliding down. He suddenly gasped as I removed my finger away from his lips and replaced it with my own daring kiss. I tasted his blood-brandied mouth and stroked his tongue with my own. Both his hands went to my face slowly touching my aching skin and I deeply exhaled in a loving sigh. He started kissing my neck while my hands slid over his healed back of scars and his lovely thundering heart. His fierce fangs pierced my neck as he brought me closer and I sighed even deeper in a lovely dream with one of his hands against my heart.

"My heart is closed. My need for you is almost overpowering but we have to forget these mortal emotions. What you seek is forbidden against my soul. Your light has been intensifying and it makes me fearful. We need to forget our hearts desires for your safety and maintain our absence." His dark inhuman voice whispered as he kissed my neck and I felt the heat of his breath heal me.

"I know I am safe with you my King." I said out of breath suddenly.

Kissing his lips made me realize how lonely I was for him. I needed his touch and companionship like my life depended on it. And even though I understood his words he didn't let me go as he kissed me heavenly embracing me.

"Thank you again for your help this morning my lovely Poesia." His voice was deep like a soothing magic and it seduced my emotions hearing him say my name out loud.

"I will always do anything for you my King." I said softly as I looked deep into the knowing of his magnetic red eyes but felt happy.

I continued to gaze in his eyes while he slowly released me and I brought my hand over his still on my heart. He was magical and he owned my treacherous heart that betrayed our friendship in lustful thoughts. And I knew it this moment he was okay with me adoring him from afar as I exhaled softly. He slowly sheltered himself with my coat and adjusted my extra fabric under my opened shirt; concealing both our outsized secrets.

Then he turned to drink his mug in silence and smelt his rose breaking our gaze. My chest hurt at my heart beating through my ribcage towards him as he sat and ate a little biscuit. His eyes lingered in mine as he offered the other biscuit. When I touched the skin on his hand the lightning in our touch surprised my fingertips and I became even more enamored with the magic of his being. His sweetness was so alluring all I could be was captivated to the gravity of his being that made me lighthearted.

"Sit Dragonfly and eat something before going about your chores. Have some of my delicious coffee. You can taste the affection I get to wonderfully taste each day." His deep voice was enchanting and that last subtle comment made me grandly blush as he smiled tenderly.

"Thank you Sir." I softly said as I sat beside him in the other chair. Breaking my devoted gaze; I looked at the little bluebirds on his windowsill singing happily in our direction.

We ate in silence looking at each other with new outlawed eyes. I didn't think about anything except being in this moment with the only man I was undeniably failing at fighting my feelings for. My hand was slightly shaking from his touch. I finished my biscuit and drank a little of the offered mug saving him the majority.

"What a glorious morning. I feel alive and full of an unexplainable vigor. Pass me some linen and I shall dress." His deep sensual voice made me sigh as I tried to forget what my heart felt.

"Yes Captain." I said and got up quickly to his old wooden wardrobe pulling out a fine linen shirt and some trousers.

I showed the informal island clothes to him and he nodded as I held them. But I turned my head as I always did when he got dressed and I only turned back when he called to me.

"Now where has my boots run off to? Pass them here." His deep voice was friendly and I smiled at his light chuckle.

I helped each boot onto his beautiful feet as he sat and lifted each leg for me. I secretly loved taking care of him and wondered if he seen it in the glint of my green eyes or my wide grin. He was smiling back and I felt like my thumping heart was lost somewhere behind the white linen, reverberating off his manly chest.

"Let us leave this dreary tower and forget our amorous feelings. A new day is upon us and we both need to greet it." He said softly as the sweet birds chirped on his windowsill and I saw his hand wave a magic green wisp around us.

He reached his hand out to me in helping me up. I nodded smiling at him while I took his gracious hand's warmth. As we moved towards the door he held my hand in a kiss and then the door opened for us.

I felt renewed but I couldn't remember why or anything else from this morning except this moment where I was walking down the long tower steps with the Captain. He moved gracefully and held a bounce in his step which made me happy. *Just another lovely day at the castle and the Captain is back to himself.* I thought as I discarded his dishes in the basin in the kitchen.

I went out into the courtyard of sunshine and merriment. Meanwhile, the Captain went about some of his outside duties to oversee some crewmen collecting wood for the fireplaces.

🌱🌱🌱🌱

CHAPTER 4

Most of the crewmen were in their mid-forties and the prime of their lives. But almost all were at least twenty years older than me. And even though I was twenty; I would always be considered a young lad to them. But I didn't mind. I smiled at the wisdom they all imparted on me. Still it was an ironic magic that the Captain be' only six years older than me and the great King of all the pirates. His full trimmed beard and hat were as broad as his muscular chest. He was considered royalty and wiser beyond his years. Even though he was younger than the men they all respected him and looked up to him; just like I did. We all had stars in our eyes for the Captain he was just too magnificent for words.

Shortblade and O'Shady had helped in rescuing us from the Royal Guard and the Captain had blessed them to become a part of our crew. But neither had defined tasks. We all had duties to complete to make the ship run smoothly and to make life at the castle easier. I loved being busy with the others. We all had the common goal of working fast so we could slag off later. We were working bees and happily gave to the hive's success.

Shortblade was new and around my age. He had yet to find his role amongst us. The Captain would pair him up with one of us trying to find out who would work best with his temperament. And everyone knew Shortblade's anger always bested him. But the Captain saw something in him and I always put my faith in the Captain.

The sun lay on Hatley over in the garden drinking rum and he waved for me to come over. I think that Hatley was my favorite of all the men. I knew he looked after me like a father would. I took a swig of the bottle and passed it to O'Shady who had been gardening with Hatley.

I was really happy at finding a couple of large potatoes when a shadow cast over me and I looked up to see the Captain's mysterious blue eyes fixated on mine.

"Dragonfly I want you to take Shortblade with you and do the linen now so they will be dry by next morn." The Captain's voice was so deep I became enchanted and blushed.

"Yes Sir." I said and nodded at the Captain that nodded back to me as well and sat beside Hatley.

They were chuckling at something and started drinking heavily. I smiled at their happiness. The castle was a place we were all safe and welcomed. And it was good to see the Captain take his Pirate Kingly crowned hat off here.

I looked over to the prima donna of Shortblade slowly getting his boots on and drinking heavily as well. *Another glorious day on the 'Isle of Fleshed Carnage' I see. I love our home even if blondie isn't in good spirits.*

"Okay Shortblade, let's gather the men's long night garments and linens. Then we can go to the river. The Captain brought back soap we can use to clean with." I said as he followed me staggering into the castle a little.

"I don't clean clothes. That's a servant's occupation." He snidely remarked as he drank more heavily from the rum bottle he brought.

"Well than you can use your big muscles to hold and gather. Once we get to the rushing river I will do the washing." I said cheerily as we started going room to room.

"I will only do it because my King has requested." He said in another sneer as he held his arms out while I piled the cotton high.

There was quite a lot and we had to make two trips. When we passed the courtyard I heard the Captain offering his aged brandy to Hatley as they laughed merrily together. *He's into the brandy deep already. That aged brandy is harsh stuff on him. I wonder what he is trying to forget?* As soon as the thought escaped my mind his blue eyes went to mine piercing my soul in grand charm and I blushed quickly turning away.

Shortblade and I hurried to the river and I quickly started washing. The truth was I didn't mind washing the clothes especially with this soap the Captain had obtained. It smelt heavenly.

"The Captain invested in this soap company in London. So we are fortunate to be able to use this over the rocks to get our clothes clean." I said as I continued to wash, rinse and ring out the garments beside the river.

I moved too fast though and my side wound opened up again as it had been doing since the Royal Guard had carved the initial of the Captain in my side for answers I would not give. We never gave them anything. My King and the pirate code was what I lived for and I would rather die than betray. I ignored my side as I knew it was bleeding and hoped it would seal soon. There would be another day I could stich the large letter. *I just don't know how.* I thought as I washed.

"What is soap anyways?" Shortblade asked and sat watching me as he drank.

"It is a chemical product using the new sciences. It is a product made out of boiling animal fat with a chemical called lye. They showed us the process after the Captain acquired the business." I said with a smile to his puzzled face.

"Acquired?" Shortblade asked cynically and then drank some more.

"Well they couldn't pay back the Captain. Anyways we have cases of this stuff. There are some also made with ash and all have hints of lavender and sea moss. It's really lovely you can smell it off our clothes and off the Captain's skin in the breeze." I said and went back to focusing on what I was doing.

"It's not normal to smell the Captain. You are odd." He said angrily as he tossed over more clothes.

"Dragonfly your eyes and mannerisms are eerie. You draw me to you and give me the strangest of feelings. And I don't know what I've become around you. I hate myself and you for feeling this way." He said as he strode away while I hummed washing the linens.

I ignored his tantrum and continued our task that we had to complete. The river was flowing greatly as the tide turned and was coming in with the mid-day sun on our backs. He strolled back to me and I looked back at the rope he strung up between trees along the shore.

"Great idea Shortblade, I usually stretch them out over the flat rocks on the beach." I said as I watched him wring out the garments and linens more before hanging them across the line.

"Yes, well I am more than my stunning good looks." He said more calmly and grabbed more of the washed cotton.

He disappeared for a little while as I almost finished. When he reappeared he had another bottle of rum and I applauded him.

"Even better idea." I shouted as he popped the cork with his perfect teeth and gave me the first swig.

"Let us truce. I wish peace between us." He said as I looked up to him and passed the bottle back.

I nodded and smiled. But I was never at war. I think it was just our petty differences and jealousy over the Captain's wanted affections. He was on our crew for a reason. And the Captain always knew best. Shortblade drank quite more than before and then passed the bottle back as we hung the last bed linen together.

"I don't know what it is about you Dragonfly. Your eyes are so different from the other men's. They are much softer as is your hands and skin." He said as he slowly discarded his shirt in the heat of the day.

I looked over but quickly averted my eyes from his rippling chest and he discarded the fancy ribbon from his hair. His long fingers ran through his luscious golden locks and I held my breath turning again away from his sensual sight.

I knew it would be one day that my features would best me in combat. My hands were much more lady-like now that I was older and it had been a terribly misfortune that my chest had been blossoming even more making it harder to hide myself.

He passed me the bottle and his fingers slowly touched mine, giving me another strange feeling that betrayed my heart. Shortblade was almost as handsome as the Pirate King but his heart was blemished with something he fought in himself. Shortblade's anger always revealed this. But the attraction between us was difficult to swallow as I only had eyes for my King and I was sure Shortblade's loneliness stemmed from his numerous declarations of missing his love.

"There is something about you Dragonfly. I cannot escape your lust even though I love another." Shortblade said as he placed his hand gently on my face and I closed my eyes from his loving touch.

I don't know if it was the wild rum or my new feelings of wanting to be held but his hand went to touch my lips and I did not waver but held my breath as his fingers brushed over my skin.

"Your lips are much softer than my lovers, as is your skin. To touch is like that of being embraced by a flower's petal." He whispered and then kissed my cheek tasting my skin with his tongue.

This was the first time anyone had ever paid me attention, unless it was ordering me around. But I turned my head towards his and kissed him as his hands went to my heaving heart in passion. I heard his gasp as both our eyes opened and his hands quickly retracted from under my shirt. I backed away from him with his shocked reaction and quickly discarded my boots and hat.

"It's just the tropical heat and the strong rum. It makes fairy magic out of mud. I think I need the icy waters." I said and ran into the freezing waters.

"We can swim if you think it will change the topic at hand but I am not easily persuaded." He said quite determined as he discarded his boots too and looked at me more intensely.

The hot sun was making me sweat and the cold waters seemed like the perfect escape. As I ran into the icy waters, I was happy to be free of the topic and his scanning eyes. I fled Shortblade further than I wanted to be though, into the rushing river. And as I surfaced my eyes went wide as the river was pulling me towards the small but turbulent rapids before the falls.

"Dragonfly the tide is in and the river is rampant. Try and swim towards me because if I can't get you now; over the falls you'll go." Shortblade's voice sounded unnaturally panicked as he swam closer to me.

His long fingers were outstretched and tried frantically to grab my hand. But as his fingers just touched mine the current swept me away. The pull was greater than the strength in my thrashing arms. I went down and up briskly to my impending doom. Swallowing the whole river it seemed as I blanked out of existence.

⚘⚘⚘⚘

I awoke and immediately turned on my side coughing and puking up water. I could feel the high sun on my bare back, as well as the person beside me that had his hand on my shoulder. His hand was heavy as it rubbed down my wound on my back and I felt horribly sick from drowning.

"Just relax and cough it out. I saved your life Dragonfly. And now I know I was right about you. You are a woman. I am never wrong about these things." Shortblade said out of breath and I noticed him wipe his dripping hair out of his face as he sat beside me.

I still breathed and coughed heavily as he patted my back harder and I felt my wound open.

"Let it out." He said still out of breath and rubbed my back harder as I groaned.

"You certainly swim headstrong like a man. That is, until the river took you." Shortblade said and laughed short from being still out of breath.

"But I don't like being deceived Dragonfly." His voice turned darker.

As I leaned heavy on one arm, my hand went up to cover my large exposed chest as I coughed up more water. His eyes were all over me and I was too weak to fight off this feeling of being a mouse caught in a fox's paw. I watch his eyes going back and forth between my eyes and my heaving body.

"These are such a delicious secret Dragonfly. I wonder what the crew would do if they knew? Actually I know what they would do.

They would string your dishonesty up to the nearest tree. You are lucky I like more meat on the bones than your tiny frame. I cannot stand this treacherous filth. I'm so angry at this deception, that I have no words." Shortblade spat out in a quiet anger as he struck me hard across the face.

"Don't worry I will kill you quickly and spare you from the rope on the tree I had made ready. But you have to pay the price for this ultimate trickery. And I will show you a great mercy that the crew won't. This doesn't make me happy in killing you, but it is the way of the world." Shortblade said as he struck me again and again.

But after getting my bearings back, I was ready to fight to live. I caught him off guard by fighting back. He wasn't expecting it as his hand went to his jaw; which I had punched hard. I undid my belt buckle and flung it to Shortblade's face like a whip. It made a cut under his eye which matched the cut he had given me. We both got up and stood there facing each other as I loosened my belt like a whip again and flung the same slash under his eye making blood spurt over his face.

"I saved your life Dragonfly. You owe me." Shortblade shouted as he slowly took off his belt.

"You saved me for what, to just kill me later?" I said as I spat on the ground some blood.

"Yes. It is illegal for a woman to pretend to be a man. You are different and should be killed." Shortblade shouted as he wrapped his knuckles tight with the leather.

Suddenly as Shortblade rushed forth, the Pirate King appeared standing in front of me. His strong back was like a shield and I could hear an eerie growl coming from him.

"You will only remember saving Dragonfly's life from the river and nothing more. You tripped and cut your face off the rocks. Now go back to camp Shortblade and have a great time drinking with the crew." The Pirate King's voice was many octaves deep and hypnotic.

The Pirate King and Shortblade were face to face. I could see his arms holding Shortblade in place; and this green smoke swirling around us all. Suddenly, he dropped his hands to his side and I heard Shortblade's shuffling feet on the rocks.

I peeked over to see Shortblade quickly leaving while placing his shirt and boots on. Shortblade left so fast that it was only a blink of a memory of what had happened; and how close I had come to being strung up in the trees for being a woman.

The Pirate King stood still with his back to me. I watched as he discarded his coat and turned his head to hold his coat out for me.

"Please take my jacket to cover your freezing body up. I have used my magic to make Shortblade forget about your secret. And your secret is safe for now." His deep voice softened as his head stayed turned from me and I shivered as I slowly took the coat.

In pure gentleman fashion he didn't turn his head to mine until I had completely fastened up the buttons. Then his concerned blue eyes went straight to the open sadness in my green eyes. Without thinking I embraced him and he stiffened at this gesture. But hugged me back very gentle.

I hadn't expected this turn of events and sat on some flat rocks beside the water as he crouched beside me. I was distraught over what Shortblade had done to my face but even more damaged by the river. I watched in sadness as the Pirate King took off his bandana and dabbed it in the water. After getting some water he wiped the blood off my face but my tears streamed down. He got more water and tried to wipe those away. His warm smile held sadness and I stilled in his mesmerizing blue eyes.

His soft blue eyes held only kindness as he continued to clean my wound and balanced his hat across his lap. The blood had been smeared as he continued to gently dab my cheek and my nose with the fresh water. He seemed so graceful that I thought that maybe he was part fairy as he exuded peacefulness. It was one of the only times I had ever seen the fierceness dissipate and worry spread across his face as he continued to wipe the bloody gash under my eye.

"My sweet Dragonfly, though Shortblade saved you. You do not owe him your life. As part of the pirate code we are all condemned to keeping each other alive and working together. If his life was being lost to the sea it would be necessary for you to attempt to save him too. We live and die by the code. And most importantly; your life isn't yours to give. You belong to me Poesia. You have since we shared our secrets over the years. I place my heart in your hands just as you have done so with me. But I continually spell us both in forgetting our secrets and my feelings." His deep voice seemed gentle but his eyes went red and glowed.

"I shall go and rip him apart now. I will eat his brains and dismember him in front of the crew. I want the new recruits to know not to mess with you or they will feel my wrath." His eyes glowed intensely and I could feel the heat off his skin with the rage he felt, even though his touch was gentle as he caressed my face.

I took his hand and kissed it. Then I placed it beside my sore face while my tears still came down.

"Our secrets must stay with each other my King. I do not wish for Shortblade's death. Please let us stay in this place of peace a bit longer. Besides, I am sorry I was not braver for you." I said softly as I closed my eyes while keeping his palm to my wet face.

"My sweet Dragonfly, tis' not your fault. I blame the heartless world that hasn't shown you any kindness as a woman; in making you hide as a man. My lovely, this has never been your fault. You only did what you could to survive and even then you almost didn't. But you shouldn't have to live in fear here. Not on our island. This is our paradise and he will have to be made accountable. His putrid heart will be on a platter before the sun sets." His voice changed to a deeper octave as I smelt the brandy off his breath.

"My King please let us keep this peace. I shall heal and maybe by then his heart will change. Besides you can't just go ripping everyone's heads off even if they are pond scum." I pleaded as my hands stayed with his on my wet face.

"Can't I?" He said and deeply chuckled.

I smiled with him completely enamored by his heroism and brushed his long black hair out of his handsome face.

"Okay, I won't kill him. But I will closely be watching. And he will never strike you again." His stunning blue eyes changed to blood red as he spoke even deeper.

My hand continued to caress his face as it softened and he closed his eyes only opening them a moment later to the serene blue I loved looking into. He leaned over and hugged me tenderly.

"Poesia there will always be people who will judge you and people who will hunt me but our strength lies in those people's ignorance. Our strong friendship can conquer any treachery because we aren't alone. We have each other and no one can take that from our souls." The Pirate King's gruff of a voice sounded soothing to my ears.

I felt his strength surrounding me and I knew I was safe in his arms forever. I just lingered in his warmth but shivered.

"We shall take the hidden entrance to get up to my tower and not bring attention. Onward quickly now; we'll go to the castle to get you warm and to get rc-dressed. I can't have you turning heads in the courtyard. You would seduce them all with your green-eyed loveliness." He said and sighed softly while sweeping me off my feet and into his arms.

"Thank you Dragon." I said and sighed too, as I looked up into his enchanting blue eyes.

"Have I ever told you I like hearing my name off your lips? Tis' music that soothes the beast and your voice is the sweetest sun-filled medley to my eternal darkness." His scruffy voice was so charming my knees went weak and I was thankful he was carrying me.

He carried me swiftly through the thick bracken and to a hidden statue in the forest. There were many wolf statues on the island placed in different locations but this one by the river and falls I had never seen before. It was covered with a thick tree moss and looked as old as the island itself. It had ancient carvings detailed into the intricate fur of the wolf. Its paws were huge and held claws that looked like it had fresh blood across.

He lifted one of the bloody claws and the whole statue slid to the left revealing an underground stairwell to a dark tunnel. As we descended the stairs the statue moved back on its own accord as if the interlocking mechanism was on some sort of invisible timer. I turned my face into his chest and away from the glowing red of his eyes that could see in the dark where there was no light.

"This is one secret entrance of a labyrinth of tunnels underground and one passage that leads to my room in the tower. I have used it many a full moon to escape." His voice seemed darker than before as he moved silently.

"Escape your family? Escape us?" I whispered as my arm went without pausing to around his middle in holding him.

"No my Pet; I would never run from my familia. I try to escape the carnage that begins after the moon is high and my thirst cannot be held back." The Pirate King sounded so enchanting but I was drained.

"Your thirst?" I asked very sleepy.

"Yes my Pet. I have an unquenchable need and desire for blood and flesh. It calls me to act upon my urges each month and the curse cannot be denied. It is also the same way your loneliness calls to me for human affection and my soul answers with the same need." His voice was a hush of deep soothing tones and I placed my hand over his heavy beating heart.

I drifted off in his strong arms as we moved down a corridor and turned a few times. Then we were ascending up a spiral staircase. I heard the loud creak of stones moving and then a heavy sliding noise of the door closing. My eyes fluttered to his room as he lay me down in his bed, removing my frozen clothes that were soaked. He covered me up with many blankets as my eyes went to his now soft blue eyes.

"Rest now. It is okay, you shall not be harmed. Wake when you are ready my Pet. I have already healed you but you must rest. I now place a spell over your heart as well as mine. This day will all seem like that of a dream including my secrets I have told you. I shall drink to forget your true beauty. I shall continue to drink to forget this day and my need to kill Shortblade." He cleared his throat and I felt his soft lips on my cheek.

"Poesia I can feel the abundant love in your heart for me. Your beauty tries to capture my heart. But it is forbidden for us to love each other. I am a danger to your mortal soul and so I shall weave a forgetting spell for us both to save our hearts from hurting and loneliness. We shall both only think of each other as great friends and crewmates and nothing more from this day forward." I heard his deep voice faraway as I fell asleep.

CHAPTER 5

I had the weirdest dream and it seemed I had fallen asleep again, as I awoke in my bed. I got up and stretched as I got up. I walked over in my nudeness to look out my tower window. I stretched a little high and opened the side wound once more as it started to bleed. But I just felt amazing from my nap and ignored the blood. The windows were so high up, that I could see men working in the garden and some collecting wood. No one could see into my window during the day and I gave another long stretch again looking out sleepily. I stopped mid-stretch as I looked down and saw the King had been looking at me with his mouth open. *It's not possible. He can't see this high up, even with his eagle eyes, can he?* I thought as I hid.

I remembered washing laundry with Shortblade and falling into the river but he had saved me. I must have been tired as I had come back up to my room for a nap. I don't even remember getting up here or discarding my wet clothes. I hastily dressed completely refreshed because the day still beckoned on this magical island. And my chores were done for today.

I was free for the rest of the day and couldn't wait to go to the lagoon. The path was a secret of the island that I always went to. The men weren't brave enough for this area of the island and did not ever come down this almost invisible trail. All of the pirates shrank at the mere thought of the mermaids. All except the Captain, which everyone feared including the lovely flesh-eating creatures.

The mermaids were vicious man-eaters, actually known as sirens. And maybe that was why I was friends with them, especially Luna. Luna was the Queen of the Sirens. She was one of my best friends and had drawn her name in the sand so I could speak it out loud.

It was the only place on the island I could shed all my clothes and swim freely as a lady. The mermaids would sing and suntan themselves on the flat rocks. Their language was only song and screams; but I felt very close to them like they were my sisters. I could tell they liked me from the beginning when I stumbled upon the secret path. Their razor blade smiles weren't menacing as they had given me free passage and friendship.

I ran to the kitchen grabbing three bottles of rum and running like the dickens past Hatley in the garden. I only stopped a mere second handing him a bottle and then fleeing the courtyard. He just waved in knowing my need for adventure and in that moment the Captain had sat down beside him waving to me too.

The lagoon was waiting and Luna. I made my way looking back to make sure no one was following me and took an unmarked path which involved swinging on a rope across a deep ravine; of which deadly fresh water crocodiles dined on the monkeys that weren't so lucky in the treetop.

As soon as I broke through the thick bracken, I ran to the multicolored sand beach where the water was a blue-green color but crystal clear. Luna spotted me on her rock and waved warmly. I grinning started waving back and discarded all my clothes on the beach. I lifted the bottles high and her yellow eyes glowed in a contagious happiness. Her smile was beaming from across the waters as I moved towards her.

I knew I was safe with her as she sang and I lay on the rock beside her. She was so powerful. It gave me great pride to be able to even share her rock with her. She was fearless as she discarded her seashells. Her skin was a lovely blue-green like the water and I wondered if it camouflaged her in their underwater palace.

She popped the cork of rum; taking a huge drink and then passed the bottle to me. I took a giant swig too and stretched out of the rock with her shimmering tail beside my bare legs. I wiggled my toes as she fanned her fins. She was simply to beautiful and magical for words and I loved being around her in the sun. We drank heavily and I tried to sing with her and then she giggled. She voice was semi-soprano and had triple vocal chords that could sing different notes at the same time. I knew I couldn't compete but I loved her melody and sang with her just as well.

We drank heartily all mid-day and swam in the refreshing warm waters. Then I took a nap on the rock while she snoozed too. I loved feeling safe around her and completely free in the sun. *What a draining day of being drown to the point that I've been so complete dreary and tired.* I drifted off in the sun as Luna held my hand.

🌾🌾🌾

I awoke to splashing sounds as I slowly got up and wiped my eyes. The other mermaids were pointing towards the forest in horror and their frightened faces made me jump into the water. I swam quickly to the shore and ran out of the water. I started frantically wrapping my busting bosom as quickly as possible. Then I threw on my shirt and vest; quickly buttoning as I listened to the rumbling of someone drunk coming out of the woods closer to us.

Luna pointed at the approaching figure on the beach that was catching me trying to find my pants of all things. For the first time I saw fear in Luna's yellow eyes as she unearthed the words; "cursed" in a hissing sound of the only English word I had ever heard from her blue lips. She screamed and went down deep into the water. While I bent down to grab my pants, unfortunately mooning the person behind me.

"Good heavens Dragonfly! Can't you keep that sausage of yours in your pants for one moment? Why are you cavorting with mermaids anyways? Don't you know they eat men like us? Maybe they like you because you haven't grown any peach fuzz yet. But you watch out, they are troublesome creatures. Now come with me Lad and fetch some rabbits for our dinner. Or else, we shall have to leave the isle and fetch some nice concubines to give in to your thirsty desires? They taste rather salty though. What do you think?" The Captain in all his gloriousness was raving drunk and though he surely be supernatural; he completely forgot all sense with the drink like we all did.

"Rabbits it'll be, and right away Sir. I'm your man." I said as I blushed.

"That's a good Lad. We will make you a burly chest-haired, fuzzy-bummed man yet." His deep voice said and then chuckled.

I rolled my eyes at that last comment and he caught me but winked. He gently passed my bow and quills. And I held his hand leading him to another path than the swinging vine to get back to the forest and castle. This little known path was full of sharp rocks and I clumsily tripped but his hand saved me from hitting the rock.

"Careful Dragonfly, I haven't been on this path in ages but I have known its treachery." His deep voice slurred a little as I turned to him and he showed a long scar on his right arm.

"Some of the rocks are laced with silver and quite sharp, so we have to be extra careful here." His deep voice slurred and made my heart raced in holding his hand to steady his wobble.

"Yes my King." I said as he clung now to my arm as we went around the ravine cliff and down some steps towards the rushing water.

The small woven bridge was slippery from the splashing river but I held the rope and the Pirate King held my shoulders as we continued through more thick bracken. He was a burly man full of a vengeful energy. He was slender but deceivingly stronger than a thousand men and was a highly skilled marksman. He could hear a fine lady's hair pin drop more than three hundred yards away and his eagle eyes could spot that pin without even trying. The Pirate King was also notorious for cannibalism and I think that was why we rarely got ambushed. He had been undisputed and unchallenged since I had come aboard almost seven years ago. But when he got drinking he was just as merry, forgetful and clumsy like the rest of us.

There was something in his exquisite blue eyes that had always made me believe he knew my secret but followed along as to not oust me amongst my companions and it was the most admiral quality about him. That was the thing about the Captain and King of all the pirates. He could smell out any deception but was loyal, until you weren't. And for those who double crossed him; even Heaven had no mercy for.

"Dragonfly where were you just now? I called you thrice." He said sternly but smiled as he stood magically in front of me; or else I really was lost in my thoughts of suddenly guessing how many people the Pirate King had eaten.

"Sorry my King." I said and focused on my task as he sat down and pulled the large metal flask out of his belt and drank some.

He handed me the jug and I took some, making the sour face after.

This wasn't rum. The Captain was into the harder stuff tonight. The aged Brandy makes you forget and you only needed a little. I always wondered why my King got so drunk on the nights of the full moon.

The meadow was easy pickings and I already had nine juicy rabbits for tonight's dinner. It was an ironic thing being on a magical island with flesh eating creatures of the night; but we had a terrible overrun rabbit population. I took another long drink as we both drank heavily and I sang him a song while I hunted. He hummed along to the tune in-between drinking. His singing voice was just as handsome as he was but he rarely showed it to anyone.

"Well I only need three more Sir." I hiccupped as I spoke and then giggled.

"Well my little daydreamer. Get to work. Of course that is why I nicknamed you *'Dragonfly'*. You would be lost to me in a meadow of flowers and sunshine. It's a good thing your arrow aim is almost as good as mine…Almost." He said in his booming gruff of a voice that held a bit of sunshine as he smiled at me passing the flask again.

"See you at the castle. Keep the brandy it helps in hunting the soft creatures." His deep voice echoed across the meadow as he turned to leave me. He took the dead rabbits with him so I could fetch the rest and in less than a blink he was gone.

It took me no time at all and so I went overboard and got nine more rabbits. *I do love pleasing the Captain. He will be so happy at our feast.* I thought as I happily drank more brandy and made my way to the castle wobbling along the dirt trail.

I had become a quick shot pretty fast. It was the only way to keep from starving. Like I had been when the Captain found me beaten to death in the street alley gutter. I was so grateful he needed a cabin boy and lock picker. And why he chose my sorrowful self, I shall never know. I was near death when he found me half-frozen and beaten. *Poor and hopeless; I was. I thought he was the Angel of Death bringing me to the other side. I wondered if he smelt my death?* I shuddered as I remembered being carried by him and surrendering to a death I couldn't fight off. I could barely remember those first days other than he stow me away in his private quarters in the Tavern and on Telulahs Revenge. And the Great Pirate King took care of me like I was his pet. I am still so grateful and would gladly jump in front of a sword for him. But I shivered again at those dark memories and continued through another field to the castle, humming to myself as I watched the dirt trail disappear.

To the random wanderer the little rat skulls would mean nothing but to us pirates the bones pointed the way to the sunken castle deep in the forest. You had to go further down to an underground cave and then come out into the thickest part of the forest. There was no path now, just partially hidden bone markings leading the way to the grand castle.

The castle was our home away from Telulahs Revenge and a sunken treasure in itself. Each crewmate had a small room on the west side of the castle. On the east side of the castle was the Captain's room high in the tower, off the kitchen. And my room was halfway up the tower stairs, which made sense since I was the Captain's assistant-willing slave.

I was grateful my room was more secluded. Since I had moved in at the age of thirteen, I had to dress in baggy clothes but never had to worry back then. But over the last few years I had to really work at wrapping and concealing my unfortunate gender with layers of ripped cloth. It was not that I wanted to be a man. It was just dangerous to be a woman in the year 1717. Pretending to be a boy had given me protection, and helped me earn a living. Nothing I could have achieved by being an orphaned, unwed woman. Even as a poor boy, I had already been an outcast living off the streets. But now, I am considered young and handsome. And as a pirate I have the family I always wanted.

The Pirate King is known throughout the seas but if you met him on the street you would never think someone as young as he would have the sole ability to take down over half of the Evil King Vermin's fleet. The Pirate King has the reputation and wisdom for being much older. His stunning blue eyes and groomed beard makes him look fierce to men. But all women desire him, tripping to be in the pleasure of his audience. He was nothing short of mesmerizing.

As I balanced the dead rabbits with my bow across my back and the canvas satchel holding my quills; I slowly walked the wooden plank bridge. I drifted my gaze down into the abyss off the side of the oak. I wondered how many hundreds of feet of a drop it was, as my foot slipped.

"Easy Dragonfly." The snide voice whispered from behind me and startled me to losing my balance as I felt a strong hand grab my arm hard.

The strong hand pulled me back to the firm wooden plank as I gasped.

"How many times do I need to save thee today? Now what were you doing on this bridge?" Shortblade said as he looked cross and sported a nasty cut under his eye.

"Nothing Shortblade; I was just looking at the deep ravine of the underground moat far below. What happened to your eye?" I said as I gulped in clearing my throat finally getting across and onto firm ground.

"Oh I fell on some rocks earlier. Looks like you have extra rabbits I see. Who are they for?" Shortblade's voice didn't hide the jealousy I ignored.

"The Captain Sir. You know he loves his rabbits juicy." I said and started towards the castle.

I could hear the music starting to play in the courtyard and Hatley singing a fine Irish medley. I smiled as I started to skip towards the laughter.

"Good job Dragonfly. But I'll take those. Go out and get some more for the festivities." Shortblade said so sinister it made me stop dead in my tracks.

"Yes sir." I said and looked in longing at the castle peeking out over the tree top.

But I handed Shortblade the rabbits and went back over the wooden plank bridge. And back into the jungle of the forest. I heard him laughing as I walked away.

Shortblade had been new and helped us escape from the Royal Guard but he hadn't been given safe passage throughout the island yet. He still needed to complete the bravery test with one night with the beast and he had respectfully declined twice now. His voice gave me goosebumps. And his eyes were always on me, watching and waiting. He seemed to be kind to everyone except me and I wondered if others knew his true nature. Luckily I had years of swordsmanship under my belt and my quiver was more true than a bluebird's breast; if he decided to take his problems out on me.

But still I was uneasy in giving him my catches. I knew he was taking credit as I clumsily kicked a rock down the trail. The one thing about the code was everyone had a job and was accountable in servitude for the greater good of us all. But it seemed I was being pushed out.

I kept my head down and went through the bracken back deep into the forest. I had finally made my way back to the meadow when the sun was setting. There was no need to go back to the castle empty handed. Without the pull of my weight for dinner I would have been going to bed hungry anyways.

Dropping my quills and bow, I ran far down the meadow to the beach of the sea. I found some rocks and threw them as far as I could. Shortblade frustrated me to no avail. *He really is a Dandy. He is far too pretty to be a pirate.* His cotton shirt was white and never held the grime of dirty suds from swabbing the deck. His long blonde flowing locks and mean blue eyes were too appealing. Even the lace ribbons that held his soft hair was too lovely.

All these strange emotions I kept bottled since he came on board, now exploded in me as I threw more rocks and stomped back to the meadow completely alone. I knew I was jealous. My hair was shorter than short; it had been since before I was a pirate. I wore a black bandana over it to hide the dark red curls that sometimes grew too fast before I could cut them off. Keeping my youth was the only thing that had kept me on the ship but I wonder if I would be able to keep up my boyish charm for much longer now that my chest was becoming even more predominate. I frowned as I looked down at my layers.

In the wind I could hear music and laughter faintly. I sat there pouting and drank from the flask as I looked up. The abrupt howling startled some deer out into the meadow as I continued to look at the stars.

The sky was lit up with twinkling diamonds that occasionally streaked by. Crewmate O'Shady said if you could catch a glimpse of the flash of light you could make a wish and it would come true. That saying always made me laugh. *What need of I for wishes? When I live such a carefree life of freedom, I have no other desires.* As that last thought came through my mind a flash of the Pirate King in the waterfall came to my mind and him flipping his long black hair. The water was slowly flowing over his bare chest and cascading down over his rippling abs. The image of him sliding his hands to unmentionable places made my breath caught in my throat.

In that last thought, I drank more of the never-ending brandy and lay in the long grass and flowers. *Why must my heart be so wretched in falling for my King? What's the matter with me? Will my dark heart ever stop desiring the Captain or Shortblade?* I drank even more in trying to drown away my strange new feelings.

My hand slowly fell to my chest as I counted stars. I listened to the crickets around me and the howling of the beast as I fell asleep at peace in the tall grass.

✿✿✿

CHAPTER 6

I was dreaming of long dark red curls and the green ribbon that I once had, that held them. I was much younger and I was playing at the orphanage. It was in kindness when the nuns had cut my hair and had given me the surgery after the first incident. They had prayed it would keep my pretty face from being sought after; by hiding me as a boy. That was another memory that I tried to forget as I listened to the howling that was much closer as I dreamt.

"Dragonfly, what am I going to do with you?" I heard his stern slurring voice that sighed heavily after.

"I know you let Shortblade take credit for those rabbits. So do the men. But you have to stick up for yourself my fair heart. The world will be cruel and you have to be stronger." The rugged voice was in a deep whisper as I felt my body being lifted into his strong arms.

His beard tickled my ear as he spoke and I had felt a smile spread across my face.

"Captain' ssso'kay, the crickets were keeping me company." I replied back and hiccupped.

We were moving fast but I could feel the wobble in his step as he shifted to carry me so that my head was on his shoulder. And my arms instantly forgot my place and wrapped around him. I nuzzled my face closer to his neck and breathed in his scent of lavender, brandy and sea moss.

"But we are your company. Stop cavorting with crickets. You had me worried the beast would find you first. Even under my protection its hunger grows for you in the darkness." His voice turned gloomy and every bit dreamier as he whispered.

His sweet brandied breath was hot on my face as I could feel him lower me gently. As he placed me on linen, my arms resisted moving from his neck and I bravely kissed him. I could taste his brandy in my mouth as he stiffened and then kissed me back more vivacious. His kisses were full of a surging passion that I knew he was holding back from.

"Sometimes, I wish the beast's hunger would consume me for I am in love with its darkness." I whispered in confession as his kisses took my breath away.

"I am the Pirate King. And in my kingdom of darkness there is no room for love." His deep voice was firm but he continued to kiss me passionately and my heart beat excitedly.

"You lie my Captain and King. I can feel it through each moving kiss of your red lips and each sweet touch of your skin to mine." I boldly whispered as I kissed him back more intense.

It was like my soul hungered to be with his even more intimately. These last years had made me notice this exquisite being as the true man I dreamt of. I could bury my feelings in brandy and rum all I wanted but I couldn't change my heart in wanting his returned love for me.

"I was not created for love. Tis' fairy magic of the island we feel. It makes the stars seem bigger and the clouds within reach. Tis' nothing more than that moonlight magic and the fine aged brandy. And even your bewitching green eyes can't weave that spell to make me open my heart for your true love. It would tame my dark soul and I refuse to be captured Poesia." His alluring deep voice whispered aggressively but continued to kiss me with an undying lustfulness.

He embraced me in one tender long kiss and then he was gone. I heard my door creak shut and I lay back in my bed in the safe walls of the castle. Immediately, I returned to slumber and started dreaming of being back in the comfort of his arms and kisses. I pulled the blanket up to my chin and turned over to the window with the full moon high.

The crickets were singing inside the darkness of my room and I smiled at hearing the werewolf raging in a howl outside the castle.

🌾🌾🌾

CHAPTER 7

The raven cawed three times as I arose ready to get the brew for my King. It was another day just like any other as my head throbbed from the brandy and I vaguely remembered my last night's dream of kissing the King. I put on my boots and headed down the stone stairs while I looked out the few tower windows and watched the pink sky. I had stretched too far again and opened my wound again. But I ignored the pain and blood; and completely went along my way in bliss.

I ran past the kitchen door to the little chicken hut of which I never saw the chickens, but yet an abundance of eggs were always found in the long grass inside the shelter. The rose bush had overgrown almost hiding the little hut now as I plucked a plump blossom and hid it under my shirt carefully. We hadn't been home in three weeks and the eggs were overflowing as I gathered over two dozen in my shirt. I carefully brought them into the kitchen while noticing Hatley watch the pot boil on the fire's grill.

"Aw, there's a good Lad. I'm going to make us my grandest of all omelets. It will put hair on your chest Boy and kick start everyone's day." Hatley was such a jolly pirate as he bellowed happily and gathered more pans and spices.

"That sounds great Hatley." I said but winced as I saw the amount of spices he was placing in a pot.

The Captain had always been an out of the box thinker and taken us around the world across oceans for the liquid treasure I was grateful for. The beans were grinded down in my mortar and pestle. Then I passed hot water from my copper ladle through my strainer filled with the crushed bean pieces and right into mugs.

The bees nest had been discovered years before and I collected the honeycombs precariously for its sweetness. I broke off a piece of honeycomb into the Captains mug daily, with his brew.

Then I rushed up the tower stairs and away from the disaster in the kitchen being made and the deliciousness of happy mistakes that Hatley was known for when combining too many spices into our food. I gently moved the large blossom to under my hat. The Captain had a soft spot for roses and it was always my pleasure to give him a daily dose of happiness.

I softly knocked on the door before entering. The Captain was still snoring loudly as he held onto his musket like it was a teddy. I smiled as I placed the mug and rose beside each other on his stand. His handsome rugged face seemed at peace as he snored. But he was covered in ash and dirt. I don't know where he had been sleepwalking in the moon's light last night, but he really was uncharacteristically filthy.

His fine linen shirt was gently placed on the back of his chair but I noticed the pants he wore had been shredded up the sides and ripped off at the bottom. His chest and rippling abs glistened in a golden color the same light shade as the honey; as the sunlight streamed through his window. His whole frame was built much different from the other men as he had no visible fat. He was pure muscle and valor. Everything about him was unusually large and I turned away as he flexed proudly through strained fabric; frightening me and exciting me.

Quietly I moved his blanket over his midriff and bare shoulders and then went to look for something nice for him to wear through his wardrobe. I slipped though and started humming a tune while I lay his clothes on the chair. Immediately I started polishing his boot buckles completely happy and unaware of the movement beside me on the bed. I couldn't help it. I lived for my King's happiness and lovingly shined the gold until it was hard to look at. I really couldn't help it. I was just happy to serve. He had given me a second chance at life and every day at the castle was a cherished domestic routine just like over the years. And I relished in these quiet times as I listened to the bluebirds sitting on his windowsill.

This day was a little different though as he sweetly snored it soothed my soul and for the very first time in almost seven years; I went to his window to see the birds. The underground cavern was the only way to get to the sunken giant castle. But the Pirate King's tower window peaked above the tree top like a giant birds nest. I slightly gasped as I saw a clear sighted view of the lagoon and meadow. I could clearly see my friend Luna sunning herself on her rock and watched her removing her seashells. *Oh my goodness. The Captain can clearly see everywhere on the island. I wonder if he has ever seen me suntan or swim with the mermaids?* I gasped as I could clearly see Luna with a merman making out on the rock.

"Oh Dragonfly, that heavenly view is not for you. You need to focus on your task and not those fair sirens. They eat men like us for dessert." The Kings voice was deep but gentle and I looked over to his wide smile as he drank his coffee.

"Yes Sir." I said with a nod and went back to polishing buckles.

"I need a swim. I smell like the wild sea serpent and the brazen brandy. And although I am parry to one of those special persuasions; I need a good rinse. Bring my island clothes, but leave my boots and coat. We are going to the river. The tide is out and the current will be non-existent." His gruffy voice said as he stood up smelling the rose and then strode across the room towards me.

He opened the door and waited only a moment for me to gather his clothes and follow him.

"Dagger too." His deep voice bellowed and then he was off with me in hot pursuit but smiling.

Down the tower steps we flew and through the long corridor of windows in the hallway that overlooked the courtyard and gardens. Crewmate Hatley was already digging up potatoes and I paused in wishing I could help my fellow shipmate garden and prep for dinner. As I passed Hatley he passed me a large flask and winked. I grabbed the liquid source of power and winked back.

"Come Dragonfly you are dragging your feet." The Captain's deep voice grumbled and slurred slightly.

"Yes Sir." I gulped as we moved past the men cheering heartily.

They all started singing sea shanties as they cleared the outdoor breakfast table and were doing dishes in the courtyard.

It always amazed me how deep the castle sat through the hollow cavern yet the forest was abundant around us. It was like the castle sat deep in a mountain that had its head and waist cut off. I wondered if it had been built like this or if it had really sunk back into the bowels of hell just like the legend suggested. The legend stated that the Pirate King made a deal with God to guard and protect innocents after all the foulness he had put forth in the world. But he had to be raised from the grave and become the matched darkness that he needed to fight.

I ran right into the King's chest and we fell to the sandy beach as my mind had drifted. I lay on him and he chuckled at our predicament. I scrambled to get off him apologizing immensely. The river sat still and the birds had stopped chirping as he strolled along the beach. This part of the river was a good deal away from the castle and very private. In general most pirates hated baths so I knew we wouldn't be disturbed for however long the King needed. Besides the river was frigid and no one liked swimming here.

"Dragonfly I wish you to come in with me. It will be good for you." His deep voice said sternly and my mouth fell open.

"Yes Sir." I said dreary.

I turned away from him when he started to discard his pants and I drank heavily from the flask that Hatley had given me. I made the sour face as I passed the Captain the flask and he drank heavily too. *Good Lord, it's brandy again. Frig it, I need it.* I thought as he took an extra-long swig and then I took another long drink.

"Do not shy away from me. We need to have this talk about the birds and the bees. I want you to see me in all my gloriousness. I am a real man and what you are becoming my Dragonfly. One day your broadsword will get bigger and your chest hair will grow in just as mine. One day you will find yourself surrounded by the femme fatale and enlarged with an unearthly lustful passion. It will be so full that the mere touch of her skin will set your heart in flames." His deep voice sounded sultry and filled with great wisdom.

But I drank while blushing even more and averted my green eyes. He stuck out his chin and puffed up his chest as he drank more from the flask too. *Brandy sure makes him forget everything. Me too though, but this is the last lecture I want from the Captain. He truly has forgotten my secret.* I pondered as I gasped. He twirled around with his arms wide in the sun completely full of an enormous romantic energy that I could feel the passionate heat off him even ten feet away.

The sun soaked in his tanned and glistening thick skin and I tried not to faint. My heart was too fair for this and I definitely didn't want to have this conversation. I drank even more, hiccupping with the Captain's hiccups.

"Dragonfly one day you will no longer be a virgin. With your handsome features you will have many damsels. But you mustn't give in to love. A women's virtue is like an enticing rose and at her center is her essence. It's her sweetest spot on her whole body. You will plunge your sword gradually until she releases and opens even more for you. But you can never rush in too deeply. You risk falling in love. I am immortal but even I can fall too deeply in love. And it would slay my beast and destroy the darkness in my heart. Never crash your sword too deep inside her soul. It would be the end of us all if we gave into our deepest desires." The King's voice was deep as he took another long drink and hiccupped.

"I have seen your stolen glances and want you to know that it is okay to be curious of your future ambitions. Right now you haven't much meat on your bones, but soon." The Captain said and as he descended into the river's calm, he wobbled a little.

"Come Dragonfly, swim with me. Shed your clothes and wash thee." His scruffy voice said sternly as he submersed under the water.

I watched him dive deeper than a dolphin and discarded my boots quickly. My only chance would be to rush into the dreaded freezing water holding my clothes in front of me. So the next time he dived I discarded everything except the thick wrapping of fabric around my chest and midriff, while he was submersed. Then I rushed into the water.

Under the water I rubbed my pants, shirt and vest together. I had been able to clean them as he emerged like some handsome merman flipping his long black hair out of his face. His golden hoop earring shimmered in the sun as his stunning blue eyes found me and he swam closer. I had kept the flask handy as I drank even more in his approach.

The river wasn't fun to swim in because of the frigid temperatures and that was why I swam with the mermaids. *But I never did laundry in the lagoon.* Making sure my clothes bulked in front of me in the clear waters; I held my clothes as he approached looking cross. I surely wasn't having fun and frowned deeply, as he swam to me with his piercing pale blue eyes.

"Dragonfly I can see you still have those thick bandages around your chest from when we were in battle a couple of weeks ago with the Royal Guard. You need to remove them. Let the water heal you." His voice was commanding and frightened me.

"Sir, I had removed the bandages only yester's eve. It is quite tedious to wrap the slice back up." I stammered out with a slight slur.

"Dragonfly I insist on seeing how damaged you were in battle. In fact I need to see the injury. We will be leaving for the sea in a couple of days and if your wounds are too great, you won't be making the journey. You will look after the castle until we come back." His blue eyes were so eerie I was worried he might know I was still injured.

I had been marked in two different spots in battle. My left forearm and pirate mark was just one injury that had healed fast considering the burned flesh. But the other wound was deep and any movement continually opened it.

"Sir, please don't make me stay." I pleaded.

"Then remove the bandages now. I demand it." His voice was deeper and commanding.

In a frustrated fit I tossed my wet clothes almost to the shore. My chest and breathing got heavier as did my thoughts as I swam away to deeper waters. I kept the flask and drank as I sank my toes in the sand under the water.

"They'll never dry that way." The Captain sighed and rushed out of the water.

He spread out my clothes on some flat rocks. Then his penetrating gaze pierced mine in such an intensity I thought he was reading the fear in my eyes and I turned away from him.

I could hear only slightly the water move. I hoped he was going to swim away and take a nice long dive again. But I felt his hand on my shoulder and jumped.

"Let's go partly in the shallows. I can see the blood through the layers of bandages on your back." He said octaves lower than normal and it gave me chills as I sighed in defeat.

He never took his hands off my shoulders as he pulled me into the shallows. We were taking steps slowly backwards together. He stopped as I stood waist deep and my back stayed facing him.

"Tis' a lot of bandages and too much of a bother, Sir." I said and hiccupped.

"I can see that Dragonfly." His deep voice seemed menacing.

"Is it really necessary to go through this hassle?" I said shaking a little.

"Yes. There we go; I found the start of the fabric. Wow, it's impossibly knotted. But don't you worry, my fangs are just as sharp as my dagger." He said quite enthusiastically and I sighed.

"Really Sir, there is no need to worry about me. I am fine." I said and froze as I heard a deep growl.

I felt his sharp teeth gently touch my side without cutting my skin.

"There we shall unravel this huge mess together." His voice held charm and amusement but I trembled at his touch.

The slice was deep around my back and I hadn't been able to stitch it but that wasn't what concerned me right now. My heart thudded so hard against my chest; I thought it was trying to flee my body. His unravelling of the extra cloth frightened me as the layers started coming off.

🌾🌾🌾

CHAPTER 8

He was unravelling the fabric as I stood still. I wouldn't risk trying to escape. There was nowhere on the island I could run to where he wouldn't be able to catch me and string me up from a tree. I tried to barely breath, thinking that would stop my heart pounding.

"Really Sir, I am more than fine." I said with my voice shaking.

"Nonsense, I know you are shy because of how tiny you are. But you are part of my crew. And I will be damned if I let you die from a hidden wound." His deep voice boomed across the river and startled some deer.

There was no one else in this place but I dared not turn around. I started shaking.

"Help me unravel will you and stop fussing." His deep voice was commanding and sounded annoyed as I quivered while he unraveled more of my layers and layers from behind me.

I held my breath as I looked at the trees across the river void of life and heard a deep manly gasp from behind me while I sighed.

"Why Dragonfly it looks like the inquisitor of the Royal Guard carved my initial into your skin. That brute was the one who whipped me with a silver sword. There begins a giant letter "D" spreading forth the length of your ribcage across to your left side. It's offensively large and deep. We'll have to look after this. Do you still have your sewing kit in your boot for emergencies?" His voice was full of concern as I shivered even more.

"Sir really, please don't trouble yourself." I said in hopelessness as my exposed top-half felt the sun's warmth on me.

I heard loud splashing and dared not turn around. Then more splashing closer and closer to me made my stomach queasy. I was still shivering from the freezing cold water as he passed me the dropped flask over my shoulder. I drank heartily and passed it back the same way. He took another long swig and gave it back. *In my worry I don't even remember losing the flask of brandy.* I thought as I tried to pass it to him again over my shoulder where one hand held me again.

"You need it more." He said in a deep whisper.

I held the flask to my shivering chest and my whole demeanor drooped while I drank more. He didn't hesitate as I felt the water splash over the open area and he began to jab me in an *in-and-out* motion of the needle and thread. I froze not because it hurt but because as the sun got higher my reflection was as clear as a painting in the water. One of his giant hands moved to my left hip to hold me steady but I was holding my breath from the frightened gasp stuck in my throat.

Everything except my hair was unmistakably feminine. I didn't have the bulk the other men had or the body hair. My arms were toned but slender and even my hands gave me away. Not to mention my tiny waistline that held the curves of an hour glass.

I was wide eyed at how close we were standing. He pulled me back even more out of the water and held onto my waist hard as he stitched. I looked at my completely exposed body in the reflection of the water and wasn't afraid as I drank even more. But I was sad. I hated the fact that I was born a woman. I longed to be like my blood clan.

In the reflection of water, I looked at his strong hand tight on my waist and wondered if that was where a man placed his hand; in dancing with a lady. I dropped the flask and brought my hands up to cover my eyes. My silent tears flowed and I wanted to hide my face from him discovering anything more about me.

"Thank you for the brandy I needed more." He said and drank heartily and hiccupped.

"Okay I need to be on my knees to sew this last bending curve that goes around to your lower belly. This will be a tender spot where the "D" curves. Be brave." His voice was compassionate as I heard the deep syllables and slowly registered what was about to happen.

I watched him drink another swig and then chucked the flask on the shore. Without warning he turned me while starting to stitch the curve that started to branch over my rib cage. With each stitch I heard his breathing changing heavier and in endless husky sighs as if he were suddenly out of breath.

Only peeking through my fingers; I noticed his left hand sewing frantically but shaking while his right hand clutched my waist and smooth stomach. As the bloody curve dipped lower so did his grip on me and his thumb found my lower secret scar that he rubbed gingerly. And I exhaled softly. My back stiffened as I covered my eyes again.

But I was tearless at what I imagined was going to happen next. It was always the same when someone found out that I was a woman. It had happened so many times before I came to the ship that I was numb to any emotional feeling behind it. The pain never lasted. But this one would, especially if I had to escape my family.

As he sewed, his other palm now lower covered me like in a shield. The electricity off his touch was fascinating and a new feeling came over me that I had never known. I uncovered my sad face and looked down to discover his sparkling blue eyes looking directly into mine. The kindness in his eyes seemed to hold a sorrow and weight in them as I looked at him past my large exposed chest. He turned me to fully face him and I felt his breath deepen on my stomach.

"Help me up Dragonfly." His deep voice sounded huskier as I extended my hand and he took it.

I held my exhale as I felt his brandy breath across my stomach when he had stood up and his hand moved to my waist.

"Come with me now." He spoke stern but all I could see was a disbelieving softness in his pale blue eyes that were fixated in mine.

He held my hand tight as led me back into the freezing water. He started to rinse the tender spots he had sewn and he cleared his throat loudly as I jiggled with the shock of the cool splashing water. Never letting go of my hand; he guided me to the shallows slowly and looked at me with a deep frown that matched mine.

He continued to hold my hand in leading me to the shore and I remained looking to the ground. A woman pirate was a great treachery and I wondered if I would ever get to see the crew or Luna again. I also wondered if I would ever see the Captain again in all his gloriousness. *I had always admired all his qualities.* I was too sad to even smile at this last thought because this was truly the end. I kept my eyes closed clutching his hand and hoped he would kill me swiftly. After all I was lucky enough to have even lived these last seven years. If he hadn't found me back then I would have perished. I had been living in a tropical paradise since and was forever grateful to have come this far.

The sounds of loud ripping noises startled me but I tried to be brave. *The Captain deserved to give me a quick death and I will not struggle.* I thought as my tears silently fell.

As I held my breath awaiting my death, suddenly I felt soft linen being wrapped around my midriff and my annoying prospering breasts. He was creating several layers over my frame and not saying a word. I was trembling still as his heavy hand rested on my shoulder where he had just knotted the wrapping.

"Put your arms high Dragonfly." His voice still deep seemed huskier than usual as I obeyed him and kept my eyes shut.

I felt him gently place the soft linen of the shirt's sleeves down my arms and over my shoulders. The fabric seemed far too nice a quality than mine and I opened my eyes to see him buttoning up his shirt over my shaking body.

"You needed my shirt. It's baggier and can hide more." He said and sighed.

"I have been in a brandied dream with you over the last year now. I have purposefully drunk the aged brandy to make me forget your beauty but today I shall never forget. The cold water has sobered me. Your birth name has also lingered on my lips in a forbidden vision that has been just as real as my return from the grave." He continued to button as he spoke softly.

As he spoke tears escaped out of my grateful eyes and I remained tight lipped. He took my hand in both of his but I still froze in place.

"Listen to me Dragonfly and let me see those mysterious green eyes. We all have secrets that we must keep hidden. My secrets are even more burdensome. But you are still part of my intimate crew and if anyone dares mess with any one of my family I shall eat them. In my drunken stupidity I have forgotten your frail past and I apologize. I drink to bury my other feelings of you and a vision that lingers of your soft lips to mine." His voice was much deeper as I opened my eyes and turned my face from his strong chest to his spectacular blue eyes.

I think I was lost in the depths of his blue and didn't say a word as the tears still silently flowed.

"I shall keep your secret if you continue to keep mine for all time." His deep voice seemed to be speaking a hidden language to my heart as it sped up.

"Yes my King." I nodded and he wiped my tears away with the softest touch.

His other hand placed mine against his broad chest and beating heart; in a pledge to me. I was weak as I looked into his eyes and more than humbled at seeing tears in his eyes for me. Here he was saving my life again just by being my friend even though he knew all my treachery. He nodded as he patted my hand against his skin that felt his wild pounding heart that matched mine and I exhaled deeply.

His eyes broke from my gaze as he looked around the beach and then left me for one moment while I stood there frozen. He came back and grabbed my hand again as he passed my pants to me. We both dressed in silence and I watched him in amazement from the pureness of his heart. Here he was the most vicious and ruthless Pirate King. He was the only man feared throughout this world and yet he showed more compassion and mercy than I ever thought existed in the human spirit. *There is simply no doubt in my mind about how lovely you are. I love you, my cherished friend.* The thought escaped me as I tried to smile but was still in shock.

"My dearest Poesia, I know my lady. There is another secret that I have, but rarely use on my own crew. I can hear your thoughts like your voice is speaking to me in my mind. And that is also the reason we never get ambushed." His gruffy voice was sultry and the loveliest song in my ears.

I blushed as I listened to his deep voice that sounded sweeter than the honeycomb I placed in his coffee every day. He suddenly smiled at me and I looked down. *I am too shy to ever admit my undying admiration. I wonder if my eyes give it away.*

"Yes, I feel it every time your green eyed magic saturates my soul as I look into the depths of your heart's eyes." He spoke while placing his hands on my shoulders and then surprisingly embraced me.

I slowly embraced him back but wrapped my hands around his bare back and lay my face against his chest while his head rested on mine. We just stood there with no time passing in the shimmering sunlight holding each other. I felt the ethereal dark magic coursing through his whole soul towards mine.

"It's okay. I know my Pet. We both have to protect our hearts from falling to deeply though." His deep voice sounded suddenly like summer rain breaking through clouds and the sun-shined passion came sparkling into my heart like a rainbow of happiness as he squeezed me.

He paused to sweetly kiss my cheek and I felt even more blessed by all the things he never said out loud. He held me and swayed slightly in the breeze as we moved like a dance in a small circle where the sun shimmered down. My eyes were closed in this fantastical real dream of a dream.

"Okay my dearest Dragonfly. I hear someone coming. Even though I drink to forget my feelings; I shall hold your secrets to my heart as you do with mine." His voice was tender in its deep tones as he gave me another tight squeeze and a wink.

He stood tall, overshadowing my frame like a wall from the approaching person as I got on my boots, bandana, and vest. The rustling of tree branches and brush getting broken made the two nearby swans that had come to the river; now take off in flight.

"Captain I have a suspicion about a certain member of the crew whose treachery knows no bounds. I believe the cabin boy Dragonfly has been stealing the treasure in the caves today." Shortblade's voice trembled as he addressed the Captain's broad shirtless demeanor.

"Shortblade you are mistaken. I have been swimming while young Dragonfly washed my clothes. The only mishap was when he brought me an old shirt. The Pirate King can only be seen in the best linens and silks or nothing at all." His deep voice boomed as I stood looking at the deep scars across his back knowing now it was the same person who carved his initial into my side.

The hatred of pirates was unmeasurable with the heartless Evil King Vermin of Bristol and it hurt my spirit in knowing they had tortured him too. I gently kissed the healed scars on his back as I hid behind his broad fierceness that continued to shield me. Then I stepped out from behind the Captain's large frame after tugging firmly on my hat. I watched Shortblade's jaw drop as I stood beside the Captain.

"Dragonfly you have your duties to attend to." The Captain's deep voice sounded dark and frightened a whole flock of birds from the trees.

"Yes Sir." I said and kept my eyes down as I hurried past the Captain and Shortblade.

Shortblade's smile seemed to have a more disturbing way about him today I noticed as I walked past him in the late-morning sunlight and carried the rest of the Captain's garments and the flask.

I hurried off and joined Hatley in the garden by the side of the courtyard. His giant orange beard was unkempt and grew like vines about his face. His eyes were green too and always seemed familiar. I noticed crewmate O'Shady had been digging out the weeds from our lustrous garden with Hatley and he gave me a small "Ahoy" from under his wide hat. Crewmate O'Shady was a new recruit too that worked hard and everyone liked immediately. He and Shortblade had saved us pirates from the Royal Guard. They were from another ship that hadn't been so lucky with the sea monster or Evil King Vermin.

"Dragonfly it's a good thing you got your arse here, I sat here pondering which veggies to harvest all morning and badly needed some rum. Can you fetch us some, so we can properly work?" Hatley's merry voice held some accent from a faraway land and I could listen to him all day every day.

"Yes Sir." I said quite jovial with a smile and rushed to the kitchen cellar.

There was nothing better than gardening drunk with Hatley. Rum always made each task easier. We did take out weeds and gather our root veggies but as the day went on Hatley would talk about the grandest of stories. One of my favorite past times was listening to him talk about the little people in the garden and of the island. He swore the little people were trying to steal his magical beard hair and use it for a roof for their small homes. He also said he had half-elven blood running through his veins and could create magic when he cooked. I loved listening to him speak of his Mum and Dad; in the happiest of stories.

Since before becoming a pirate I was an orphan; but now I lived for the new family I had. The only memory I had was of the nuns telling me the surgery was for my own good so I wouldn't have any more unwanted babies. At the time I didn't know what it meant because I had always wanted a big family. I ran away as soon as I was healed and then found out the real cruelty of a man's world. I don't blame the nuns they had showed me a kindness. And out of that kindness I was able to be a part of the grand family I had today.

I got several bottles of rum. Today's day was going to be one of the best. But before I left the cellar I re-filled the large flask full of brandy. Maybe I could forget this mid-morning and just move into the sweet slumber of tonight that I wished would speed up the hours of the sun. I tucked the flask in my belt under my shirt and rushed back into the happy courtyard.

CHAPTER 9

I turned back to Hatley as each of us had our own bottle of rum and mugs. Hatley had been swatting away a small orange butterfly attracted to his beard it seemed. Whimsical as that moment seemed; was only a spark of the magic surrounding Hatley. He would drink from his bottle and the butterfly would flutter its wings but not leave. It was like some enchanting fairytale. Clearly the butterfly was in love with him.

"Do you see that? This little bloke is trying to steal the rum from my beard. Dragonfly get me' gun so I can blow his bloody head off." Hatley said as he tried to shoo the fluttering butterfly away.

"I think that won't be necessary my good friend." The Captain's deep voice seemed comical and I saw his grin spread over his handsome face.

"Yes Sir Captain. We were just gardening." Hatley said as the butterfly was lavishly fluttering its wings in the bright orange of Hatley's beard.

I drank heavily from my mug and laughed at Hatley turning red. I looked down and dug out some nice potatoes for our dinner. The giant spuds I had found were huge and drank quite more in being pleased with myself for finding these buried treasures.

"I'm sure you have been working very hard but I need Dragonfly to fetch us some rabbits for dinner." The Captain's stern voice seemed spookier somehow and I looked over and nodded.

"Yes Sir." I said and wobbled to the castle as the ground seemed to be moving past my feet.

As I fell I laughed and heard Hatley roaring with laughter and it seemed his great belly shook with happiness. I looked over at him from upside down. He had tipped over in being jolly and I watched the Captain helping him up. I had gotten up and brushed myself off. And even though the earth had been tilted; I got to the back door of the kitchen. Before I stepped through the door I heard the Captain and Hatley's loud voices.

"Get my gun this butterfly is trying to eat me face off. Quick." Hatley shouted.

"I think you are in trouble my friend. It's far worse than that. I think that little bug is in love with your beard." The Captain's deep voice boomed over the courtyard and then he chuckled.

"Quick save me my Captain. Get my gun. 'Tis a fate worse than death." Hatley pleaded as the Captain chuckled.

"Oh Hatley. Give me some of that rum." The Captain's happiness was contagious as everyone in the courtyard laughed too.

I giggled as I wobbled past the kitchen and then to the throne room and long table where my bow and arrows were always kept by the Captain's chair. Shortblade was dangerously sitting in the Captain's chair eating an apple with his shirt unbuttoned and his boots dangling off the side of the wood.

He purposefully kicked my weapon to the floor as he saw me approaching still giggling. Even that distasteful show couldn't wipe the smile off my face or laughter from my voice. I hummed now and gathered everything off the floor.

"Where'd you think you're going with such a pretty grin?" Shortblade said snarky.

"Just chores." I said hiccupping but still smiling as I clumsily staggered from the long room into the kitchen and felt a tug of my shirt behind me which sent me backwards to the floor.

I laughed as Shortblade sat on me and pulled his dagger to my throat.

"I could kill you right now and no one would care you little nose-picker." He snarled as I felt the sharp blade touch my skin.

"You could and I wouldn't feel anything but happiness, as you can see my nose is rather clean." I said and laughed.

"Get out of my face. You don't belong here you know. You are too merry and pretty to be a pirate. Everyone knows it." He spit beside my face but it sprayed me.

I laughed as I wiped it on his pant leg. He couldn't hurt me. The rum gave me extra invincibility and a new magical strength that even he couldn't break. I laughed and got up gathering my stuff again as the floor wobbled with me. I looked back at him and noticed his sad face.

"Why don't you come with me Shortblade and have some fun." I said as I wobbled to him with my hand extended.

"You wouldn't understand. I feel lonely like this castle is actual a casket that separates us from the sea and the ones we love." Shortblade said as his voice changed from anger to a deep hurt.

"Then let us be the ones you love. Instead of despising us, join us and be merry. We have each other." I said as he let me take his unwilling hand and gently pull him to come with me.

"Why are you forcing me Dragonfly? Why this kindness? I know I don't deserve it after I have been rotten to you." Shortblade said and turned me so fast I was falling but he caught me.

"Everyone has a broken heart here, but we also have each other. I believe in you Shortblade and under that mean mask is a kind heart." I said as he helped me up.

Without any words Shortblade let me take him to the courtyard and he sat with Sully; joining a large group. I waved to the large group in the garden who were laughing and being merry. Crewmate O'Shady was telling a story about a Dragon King that used to live on this very island and I watched as some of the men's eyes went wide.

I noticed the Captain staggering back into the castle and I followed him as he wobbled down to the cellar. He looked like he was having a difficult time as he tried to get some brandy off the shelf and I touched his back making him jump.

"Oh Dragonfly you startled me. I was just after some more aged brandy." His deep voice said as he wobbled.

"Sorry Sir, I just wanted to help you." I said blushing as I wobbled and got the bottle for him.

The Captain suddenly was falling and I tried to catch him but instead we fell together on a burlap sack of flour. It puffed in a white mist as we laughed in our drunken state. He pulled me into his arms to help me up and instead we fell together crashing back on the flour. He broke out in laughter and so did I in our misfortune, as he lay on me. His face was really close as we laughed and he paused looking into my happy eyes. He placed his hand gently to the side of my cheek and smiled so warmly at me. His eyes were the most dazzling blue and he brushed his fingers across my cheek. He looked deep in thought whereas I didn't have to contemplate anything. I reached my hands to his face and pulled down his smile to mine. I know I was being bold but the liquor made him look even more magmatic. He paused only a moment from opening his mouth to mine and stroked my tongue in a dance. His hands caressed my face. But my hands had untucked his shirt and slid underneath the cotton while we kissed. My hunger for his mouth seemed to be growing as he ravished me with kisses and gently stopped my hands from going further.

"Dragonfly, we can't keep losing our senses in our loneliness. I have duties and you have duties. I am a King. We need to try to get up right now or else I might fall for you even more than I already have. Please let us leave our love and this room." The Captain's deep voice was out of breath and he paused in kissing my hands.

He slowly helped me up and we clung tightly to each other's bodies as we made our way up the cellar stairs. But before he opened the door, I pushed him gently to the wall and kissed him with such ferocity in my soul it frightened me. And I noticed he held me tight with his eyes closed in kissing me back just as fervently. When he opened his eyes they were contented but red. As he kissed my neck I felt his fangs pierce my skin in a lovely euphoric heat. His eyes now held a look of surrender as he sighed irresistibly and I gasped at being somehow up against the wall. He kissed me gracefully as he adjusted our clothes back to regularity and healed my neck with his hot breath. Then he passed me the large golden flask once again that was full.

"Take this brandy to help you hunt swiftly." He said and then kissed me again.

"But Dragon what about your needs?" I said and placed his hands over my heart.

"I think I shall be okay but missing your presence as you hunt." His deep voice slurred as he revealed another brandy flask in his large coat pocket.

We lingered on the staircase in more stolen kisses and then walked out of the cellar together. I grabbed my waiting bow and quills as I wobbled into the courtyard and then the Captain stepped out moving swiftly towards Hatley.

Meanwhile a smaller group was drinking and laughing in fascination at the butterfly still attached to Hatley's orange beard. The Captain had hit Hatley hard on the back making him spray out rum and the butterfly briefly flew off but then re-attached itself.

"It is true love Hatley." The Captain chuckled deeply while everyone laughed.

"Like hell it is. Why won't anyone get me my gun? I'll remove this little freeloader once and for all." Hatley spoke frustrated as he punched himself hard in the face and toppled over.

As Hatley fell into a very brief slumber the butterfly flew up and then went back to its new home in Hatley's beard. Everyone roared again with laughter as the Captain tried to help Hatley up while chuckling.

"I have an announcement. I have invited some guest's to the island. Please men, show the women an inviting time but make sure they don't leave the castle grounds after nightfall or else they will perish at the beast's claws. I received their confirmed reservation by message in the bottle today, stating they will be here after the full moon. This should be later today. I know you shall keep the good ladies safe in your rooms at night." The Captain said and lifted his waiting mug as all the men raised their mugs in cheers and hollers.

I cheers with the men but my eyes were drawn to the Captain's eyes that had scanned the crowd and stopped on me. His smile was wide with his fangs exposed and the men seemed too drunk to notice that the Captain was slightly exposing his darker side but I watched as the red flashed through his blues. The Captain had other motives for inviting people to the island and I knew it as he smiled at me. I held my waiting mug up but my smile faded as his fangs got longer while he looked at me. I knew he was inviting his next meals to the island. *I can't believe he is showing his fangs. He must really be drunk this time. I wonder if I am in love with not an angel, but really the Devil hidden in plain sight.* I shuddered at that thought as I left the party and music that had started up as everyone drank and laughed heartily.

I passed the stone wall of the courtyard out of sight and slowly made it over the plank boards that seemed to be moving sideways with the world. I could hear our favorite sea shanties in the background as I got the flask out and stumbled into the jungle of the thick forest.

As I made my way to the meadow I saw the boats already up on the beach. Our company was already arriving with the ladies of the night in many beautiful dresses and satins with showing fishnet stockings.

The Pirate King had invited his longtime friend who provided the disposable women and men. Cut-Throat Kathleen had been a dark heart since the day I met her. She was paid well to keep the brothel on the outskirts of Bristol, for the Pirate King. She had employed all kinds of ladies and men for years now. Especially intriguing was how they all were the loving kind of ladies and men; but some longed for death. I had seen this many times over the years and tried not to think about the dancing spell the Captain would weave on the party tonight at the masquerade ball.

It always astounded me how people would come willingly to sacrifice themselves to the beast, a haunted castle and an island where the Pirate King inhabited. The visitors were always given warnings but yet they would slip away in the night.

I would say that the graveyard on the island was small but that would be a lie. The only small truth lay in that the bodies that were buried were never whole. The bones lacked something other than a beating heart and shredded flesh. The beast didn't leave much of the corpses and the caskets were never full, so the men didn't bother with them anymore.

CHAPTER 10

I barely made it over the planks with the twenty-three dead rabbits; I balanced just coming back into the courtyard of cheers. I was happy too, seeing that I was a better shot drunk it appeared. The women were already scantily dressed with certain crewmen. They sat on burly laps being the lovely creatures they were with skin showing and chests that spilled out of their over-bust corsets. I knew what the women did as a profession but they still seemed like fair ladies and I refused to call them by the *'concubine'* name the crew had given. They still had a heart in their chest and were brave souls. I knew how hard it was for an unwed woman on the streets and I wasn't about to make their lives any harder.

The Pirate King had strict rules about the ladies and it made me feel better knowing none of the women were to be abused; only shown a good time. It was like having a last wish of a pleasurable time especially the ones who wanted to die. I drank in that knowledge that was bestowed on me from Hatley years ago. Some fellow masked crewmen had helped me in taking the rabbits to another section of the courtyard. I could see they wasted no time in skinning and impaling the now fur-less creatures and sticking them over the large bonfire pit. The courtyard had turned to a masquerade-themed ball with people dancing and musician's playing strange tunes from across the seas.

The floral decorated party was set far in the courtyard and away from our beloved garden. Some crewmen were singing around the fire as I walked past to the castle. Ladies would smile sweetly towards me and wink. I know Cut-Throat Kathleen had told them I was a virgin and although I was flattered; I only had eyes for the one man that ruled the night.

The Pirate King was wearing his best for tonight's affair. He had his hat and coat buckles 'gold gleaming. Everything about him seemed more dashing as his heavy boots seemed lighter than air in dancing with one fair maiden. Everyone including the maidens was drunk and I carelessly watched in longing at the Pirate King dancing with the lady. Her red dress flowed to his movements as he twirled her around the courtyard. My cheeks turned red when his eyes shifted to mine and stayed with me through each twirl. I turned suddenly away from his intense stare and I exhaled heavy through the kitchen door.

I went back to the Pirate King's chair in the long room, where I delicately placed my bow and quills. I remembered earlier where Shortblade had threatened me and felt the painful slice under my chin. I chuckled at the small amount of blood on my fingers and shook my head as I went down the corridor to the cellar.

The cellar was a dark place for guests and crewmen to go so I didn't linger as I filled my flask with brandy and ducked in the shadows under the stairs as people were coming down.

I noticed instantly the long blonde hair's lacy ribbon being undone.

It was Shortblade and he was being pushed up against a wall kissing someone quite aggressively. His eyes were closed as one of Cut-Throat Kathleen's servants started twirling his golden locks in their fingers. They both drank deeply from the same bottle of rum completely enthralled with each other, in kisses and hands that frolicked all over their wanting bodies. They seemed to be completely absorbed with each other's company and oblivious of me as I stayed hidden but in view of their secret show. Up until this moment I had never noticed Shortblade happier and in love before. The servant was slowly removing articles and throwing them to the side while Shortblade kissed them. The servant had also been slowly undressing him as they drank. I held my breath in seeing Shortblade naked and aching from the servant's hands.

Shortblade's eyes remained closed as he kissed the servant back ardently and his hands went everywhere. I placed my hands over my mouth and waited for a moment in this heated desire to make my escape. After long moments of kissing and passionate movements; the servant was now forcefully crashing into Shortblade and ruthlessly making his handsome mouth moan loud in a heated ecstasy. A sound I had never heard from Shortblade's vulnerable mouth as he then screamed in passion. The servant was relentless in not letting Shortblade catch his breath and I gasped at the pleasurable torture.

I slowly made my way up the stair's shadows listening and watching the two lovers as they then lay on the giant flour burlap bags in the corner. They held each other both breathing heavy and exhausted. Laying naked in a warm embrace of slow kisses and moving hands. The sweet murmur of true love was the thing I lived for and I couldn't help but stop to watch and overhear their whispers of adoration.

"I love you and everything about you Robert. You were carved from the finest pearls and diamonds of all the seven seas." The servant said as he held Shortblade in his arms kissing him sweeter than I have ever seen anyone being kissed.

"I love you too my beautiful Philip. I need more of you. You have to promise you will come back to the kingdom with me. I could not rule the lands without you by my side. I am so in love with you." Shortblade said softly as he kissed Philip deeply and Philip continued to caress him.

"Yes is my answer. That's all my heart thinks about and these hidden moments with you. Well that and more hidden moments with you. You are the love of my life after all." Philip then completely moved behind Shortblade kissing the back of his neck ever sweetly.

Philip was holding Shortblade in his arms while they kissed in complete tender vulnerability.

It made my heart swell as I wished the Captain could hold me in his heart that fondly. But just like these two star-crossed lovers; I wondered if it could ever be. *Could there ever be an earth where we could all exist as ourselves? Or would we all have to hide our love away from the world?* As my thoughts escaped the stair step creaked.

"Quick get dressed someone is coming. We cannot be caught or it will be our necks." I heard Shortblade say sharply as I ran up the stairs and slammed the cellar door loudly.

I had the three bottles of rum of which I had come for and my flask filled with brandy as I tried to run out of the castle. I ran into Hatley as he was just coming through the kitchen door.

"Oh there's a good Lad. You read my mind. I needed another bottle. Come with me." Hatley said as I followed him out and noticed Shortblade coming up the cellar with Philip close behind.

Hatley had not seen the gushing pair come up from the lower level. But I caught them holding hands as they closed the cellar door and Shortblade had given me a look dropping Philips hand fast. As I closed the kitchen door, I saw them move to the west side of the castle where the crews' rooms were. And Shortblade continued to watch me with a deep frown as Philip took his hand once more.

I took a deep breath of the night air as I joined the festivities in following Hatley to the fire pit and the sun was setting. The music was still going on and the Pirate King was still dancing but now with another lady in a frilly indigo dress that revealed a lot of beautiful curves. He was handsomely laughing as I walked by and I took another swig of the flask. I could feel his captivating blue eyes on me as I passed him.

Hatley had saved me a spot by him around the bonfire and a mask. He had some hearts, legs and biscuits for me saved on a plate which he offered to me for dinner. As I ate, we all sat and listened to ghost stories of the island. I looked behind me to the shadows of the wall where the Pirate King had sat with the lady. Her hands were moving over his now exposed muscles atrociously as they kissed and I looked on with a sour face. He caught me looking at him just now and I turned away frowning.

I focused on the stories and the laughter of the crowd as crewmen were slowly slipping into the castle. Somehow we were on horror stories of how Hatley had lost his virginity three times when he was a young man. But everyone was laughing as he explained about one time when he was much younger he had dated a one legged, one eyed-hooker named Francesca. Who he later learnt was a man and still went with it because he had paid a good amount of gold. Others were roaring at Hatley in teasing, while Hatley smiled wide.

"Hey, I paid to be serviced with my gold." Hatley said with his larger than life smile.

"Jeeze Hatley, even Hairy Henrietta is prettier than Francesca." Crewmen Sully said and laughed.

"That be' true about a lot of hookers. But Francesca has no teeth." Hatley said and laughed quite jovial as his belly shook and one of his buttons popped off his shirt.

"Aye." All the men cheered and raised their glasses.

CHAPTER 11

I toasted the men in cheers too of the mug Hatley had for me but had no clue what the men were talking about. Hatley was in good spirits even with his beard taking up a resident. The orange wings slowly fluttered through Hatley drinking and kissing his lady companion.

I turned to see the Pirate King kissing another lady and his hand was dangerously on her exposed thigh showing her stockings and crinoline. I blushed as he looked over at me and turned around quickly. *I need a good plan as the night grows longer. We all have been drinking heavily including the Captain and the brandy is making me think I could do that too. The ladies all have wigs on and their masks hide their identity well.* With those last thoughts I drank the last of the large flask I had and ran into the castle to where the unpaired ladies rooms were. Picking the lock was easy as I stole a lavender dress, wig, corset and lace garter to hold the stockings I wouldn't be wearing. I would be barefoot but I'm sure the Pirate King wouldn't notice by now. I also grabbed a bottle of brandy and then rushed to my room to change.

I dressed in the scantily clad lavender dress that revealed the curves I wanted him to see. My chest heaved in breathing so hard out of fear as I slipped my mask back on and attached my beautiful white wig with pins. I had painted my face and cleavage as white as the other ladies did and used the rouge to coat my lips to the blood red color he loved. As I looked in the ancient mirror I gasped at how beautiful I was with this fake hair and makeup. My chest was bubbling almost out of the over-bust corset and they looked so full you could sink your teeth into.

I smiled at myself while carefully drinking a huge amount of brandy and went out the castle a different way. I paused in the moonlight just at the wall to the courtyard where the music and singing played on. I had to pause because my heart felt like it was going to beat through my chest as I wished for my King to see me beautiful.

"My dear delicate lady. What are you doing unaccompanied outside the castle wall? Where you not told of the beast that prowls the island at night?" Shortblade's voice sounded upset but he was courteous to me.

"I'm sorry good sir. I got lost and was just coming back." I said and made my voice a higher pitch.

"I gently warn you to not let it happen again. Please let me escort you my dove." Shortblade said and bowed as he kissed my hand and escorted me around the corner of the courtyard.

The Pirate King was dancing with a lady in a very translucent yellow dress with no corset and my mouth opened in shock as I looked around the courtyard where men were making out with partially dressed ladies. I gasped at the scandalous scene. Shortblade didn't miss a thing and whispered as he held me tight in a grip.

"I know who you are. Your green eyes are a dead giveaway. They sparkle and are too unique. I also know it was you who had caught me with Philip." He whispered coldly and then started to dance with me around the courtyard.

Suddenly, the Pirate King aggressively tapped Shortblade on the shoulder.

"I demand this dance. Shortblade, you can have my dance partner who wants to retire to your quarters." The Pirate King's deep voice said and Shortblade nodded smirking as he took the lady away.

"I have not seen you with the others." The Pirate King's deep voice was gentle but firm as he took me in his arms to waltz.

He danced nobly while the music played on. The Pirate King was in fact a pure and distinguished gentleman. I think that was why I and other women drooled over him. I smiled politely as I looked lovingly into his eyes.

"I am new to Kathleen and shy. So I hid in the shadows." I said and looked down as he studied me and smiled.

"You are too beautiful to hide away and I would know if I had seen you sooner because you'd not have been with such an inadequate dance partner." His deep voice remained gentle as he twirled me and smiled.

"In fact if I had seen you sooner, I would not have let you go. Your green eyes are like emeralds and they shine brighter than all the diamonds I have collected. You are too graceful and lovely to be in this profession. I wish I would have found you sooner. I am a King but you steal my breath, in your powerful gaze." His deep voice seemed to be seducing my heart as I danced with him.

We gently laughed together as he made some jokes and I hung off every gorgeous note of his sultry voice. He gently twirled and dipped me low. And as one song ended he stole one soft kiss on my neck. As each new song began and ended he danced only with me. As I grew out of breath from the heat and our dances, he offered me his arm as we moved to a different place in the shadows of the courtyard.

"My lady I have not the daintiness that you deserve in a sweet aged wine but I hope that you would share with me this hundred year old brandy as a token." He said softly as we sat on a little bench out of view from the fire and other dancers.

He passed me a golden flask and as he touched my hand the same shocking sensation went through my skin and I saw his eyes flutter as we were zapped. I drank heavily from his offered flask as he moved my long wigs hair out of the way of my powdered cleavage.

"You are too magnificent and irresistible for words. Your sensual charm gives me a feeling I cannot express. Please give me your name or I shall die a thousand deaths." His voice seemed huskier as he looked into my eyes and then drank heavily of the brandy.

Even though we were both drunk; I wanted to stay in his mind and heart for all eternity. I hoped he would remember me this fine-looking. And I hoped he remembered that I took his breath away.

"My name at birth was Poesia." I said sweetly but I had meant to lie and not give him my real name.

His hand held mine delicately and he pleasantly leaned down to kiss with his tongue tasting my skin. I held my breath again as he kissed my hand once more and then placed his hands on the side of my face brushing the white wigged curls away from my eyes.

My breath got stuck in my throat as he leaned over and kissed my lips with the full force of his being. Tonight he wasn't holding back. I felt in each kiss the hunger and fever coursing through his veins. And suddenly his eyes opened wide into my green eyes.

"Let us go my graceful lady to someplace less crowded." His voice was huskier and much deeper as he offered his hand and arm to me.

We quickly moved out of the courtyard and to the other side of the wall out of view. The moon was high in the sky as he pressed me against the wall with passionate kisses and the heat of the night was getting to both of us as his coat and shirt were open. I could see the light perspire all over his strong clavicle and down his very muscular chest.

"Your soft lips are so elusive it is like they have never experienced true love before." His deep voice was soothing but that last comment made my heart hurt.

He was right. I was obsessed over the Pirate King like all the other women and never really knew if he ever returned my affections. I knew he didn't mind but he never openly declared his love or any other inclination to make me think he felt the same way. I turned away from his wanted desires just then as my unloved sadness got to me.

"I am so sorry. Did I say something to offend you Mon Cherie?" His deep voice was full of concern.

"No, I'm sorry. I was just thinking of past situations and how timid I have ever been to act on what it is I want." I said softly and looked away.

He offered me more brandy and I took quite a lot more. I didn't want to be sober and feel the rejection that might come. He was drinking heavily too and stopped to gaze his deep blue eyes into mine.

"What is it that you want Poesia?" His deep voice was even more glamorous as he spoke my true name on his lips.

"I want you. I always have." I said slurring my words slightly and then fiercely kissed him into dropping the flask.

"I want you as well. I have since the moment I saw you. But will you still want me tomorrow?" His seducing slurred voice answered back and enticed me by kissing me slowly behind my ear moving down my neck.

Then I kissed him just as sweet as honey. His hands went to my bodice and started trying to undue the impossible over-bust corset as my hands pulled off his coat and shirt that were almost off anyways. I giggled as he chuckled and he used his dagger to cut the wretched corset from my bodice. Our masks stayed on as we kissed and his hands found the lace garter but no stockings.

"Mon Cherie, you have no boots and have been barefoot all this time? You are a true empress after my own heart. The formalities are beneath us when two hearts become one." His voice slurred warmly and was inviting as he gently picked me up.

He took me to his private rose garden. The sweet grass was the softest pillow as we slowly kissed. He gently moved me down to the plush greens that were surrounded by the allured scent of luscious roses plump and deep pink in the moonlight. I liked the fact we still had our masks on as we kissed. We were both in this scandalous dream of moonlight and brandy. I couldn't get enough of my King and he wasn't holding anything back tonight. He covered me completely full of voracity. Our bodies in motion like the gentle rocking of the ship in the harbor. He was gentle but his exuberant passion coursed through my quivering soul. And I hungered for him as I needed more with the moonlight highlighting us both in this secret grove. His hands and mine were interlocked in some magic spell that broke out into the garden of little lights as fireflies flew all around us. I opened my eyes to see his closed as he kissed me. I looked past his shoulder in the heat of the moment and seen abundant red velvet roses blooming. There was this magical green wisp surrounding us as he moved deep and I was grateful for the music loud in the distance as I sang out while he howled. Our sounds together were otherworldly as he collapsed on me and we both caught our breath.

He whispered in my ear a sweet kiss; "I have been so lonely without your wanting arms and warm heart against mine. I have waited for you for centuries."

🌱🌱🌱🌱

CHAPTER 12

I awoke snuggled warm in his arms and from behind me he shifted with me in a scandalous dream. He moaned softly as he lightly dreamt. *So this is what heaven feels like.* I smiled as I opened my eyes and then silently gasped that we were in his room in the tower. My dress and his clothes were across the room over his chair with the sunlight shimmering down on my wig. My head hurt but this feeling of euphoria came across my trembling body as I felt him again shifting behind me. *Good heavens, he feels so good still intensified with his awakened raw passion.* I indulged in his sweet kisses down my neck and he moved us feverishly matching my insatiable need. Suddenly he moved over me with his undying lust deeply direct as he kissed me longer with his eyes remaining closed. I wanted more of last night and our secret romance.

I looked over his shoulder as I was moaning and seen the roses I had brought him days before. They had been dying and were now coming back to life more effervescent than ever with this green wisp of magic surrounding us. As he finished he buckled on me in even more sugary kisses. After this beautiful awakening, his heavy breathing slowed as he held me in a body-hug and whispered; "I have always loved you Poesia."

He held me so tight while he easily went back to snoring softly and I whispered back; "I love you too."

⁂

Just like a heavy dragon guarding its treasure I awoke again with his leg and arm draped over me. I softly yawned as my head ached. I looked over at our clothes across his chair once more in the shimmering sunlight. Silently I gasped again as I realized both our masks were now off as he lay holding me. I slowly moved his arm off my body and gently moved his heavy leg back. Very quietly, I covered him up with the cool linen sheet as he snored. But as I removed my arm back from him, I felt him gently grab my hand.

He sat up suddenly; still holding my hand and with his other large hand grabbed his head. His deep blue eyes glazed over me and our clothes across his chair. Both masks were in the sunlight beside my wig.

"Dragonfly, my head hurts treacherously." He whispered but did not let go of my hand and I tried to still my beating heart and gasp.

"You and I were not ourselves. But dressing up and seducing my intentions is a mutinous attack on my heart Dragonfly. What were you thinking? What if someone seen that it was you in disguise?" His deep voice was soft but aggressive as his steel blue eyes looked deep in my soul.

My head hurt too much for this conversation and I couldn't stop my tears as he held my hand gently but refused to let me go. Quickly he got up as he held my hand and towered over my small frame in the sunlight.

His muscles flexed and glistened with the sunlight. He was breathtaking even though I was caught. His questioning alluring blue eyes weren't blinking and mine were pleading in a useless tear-filled pool of droplets running down my face. His breath slowed as he waited holding my hand for a response from me and I took a deep inhale before my hearts confession.

"I thought you would think me more endearing, if I was beautiful like the other ladies." I said and covered my wet face with my free hand as I could still feel his eyes over me while my heart was exposed in the light.

I held my breath as he surprisingly embraced me.

"Do you really think the wig, and dress made me affectionate towards you? Your beauty has always lain deep inside your bountiful chest, my dear Poesia. No amount of rouge can make a diamond sparkle more. It glows from within. And that is your glittering soul that shines in the darkness, letting my dark heart find you each time." His deep voice was soft as he slowly swayed me in his arms with my wet face against his bare chest.

Our bodies were warm and exquisite together as my eyes closed in savoring this moment where we slow danced. I don't know if Dragon could feel it or not, but my unadorned heart fluttered in response to his tenderness. I could certainly feel his responsive touch as his heart thudded against my ear.

"Last night was just moonlight magic and our equal loneliness." He softly said as he placed his hands caressing both sides of my face.

His magmatic blue eyes were so enchanting as I looked back into them that I felt like I was falling as he kissed me slow, deep and true. Then unexpectedly, more of his sweet kisses came flooding through like a summer rain, light and warm all over my body.

He gently carried me in his arms back to the bed while I held onto him with all the love in my heart. This time as the sunlight dazzled down there was no mistaking anything as he kissed me and kept me in his arms while we made love.

❦❦❦❦

"You know my lovely Pet that I am a King and I have duties to our home and our crew. As do you. We cannot have any more stolen moments. This will be the last time our love can be in the sunlight. We have to hide it. We cannot just give into our fantasies anytime we want or else we would only have this enduring love for all time. This is quite impossible and quite treacherous." His deep scruff of a voice whispered as he kissed and cuddled me even more.

I nodded and whispered in response; "Yes, my King."

We were kissing each other without holding back from the love we needed and were enraptured with each other a thousand fathoms more of unabashed excitement. It was as if the words came out of my mouth and suddenly I was swept in another wave of our bodies rolling, hands grasping, sheets twisting; and lip biting delicious seduction. The birds were singing and so were our souls in the ultimate happiness of sunshine bursting forth from our panting heated-bodies.

❦❦❦❦

CHAPTER 13

I felt in a lovely waking dream where a wish had come true and I found my chores seemed lighter. I was plain old Dragonfly as I emerged into the courtyard but I felt different. The chores were never really hard to begin with as the brimming sun was high. Hatley had been sitting drinking rum and telling some of the other crew about the howling he heard last night. I giggled with the other men's burly laughter.

"I'm telling you the Pirate King created a storm off the east of the island and when he exploded; Telulah emerged with rage. My heart goes to the Lass he gave it to. It was probably her last moment alive." Hatley took off his hat and placed it over his heart.

"Aye. She isn't with us anymore. That'd be true. I found the discarded yellow dress outside the courtyard wall this morning." O'Shady winced as he spoke and brought the yellow see-through dress out.

I looked at the dress and remembered the sad lady that wore this see-through gown. I wondered where she had gone. *The Captain was with me all night and she went with Shortblade.* I thought quite puzzled as I looked at the dress holding the fabric up in the light.

"Give me that Dragonfly. We need it for the burial." Shortblade snatched the dress from my hands and shocked me as I didn't even know he was there.

"The beast had fed on at least three. Why do we put up with this creature of carnage? There are enough of us here that we could hunt and kill it." Shortblade shouted.

Hatley being a peaceful man did something I had never seen before. He stood up taller than Shortblade and slapped him hard across the face. Shortblade actually smiled after even though the large red handprint was visible across his face.

"Listen for those of us who passed the bravery test, the beast protects. The beast saved us from marauders a few years back while we were sleeping. I will not have you talk badly about the werewolf. It is needed." Hatley shouted back in anger.

"I have seen the body Hatley. The monster ate her gizzards, everything was torn into. Her insides were torn to something resembling string. This can't be right." Shortblade said and turned away from us and into Cut-Throat Kathleen's mad face.

"You fetching blonde-man idiot, did you even know her name? Because I knew Maddie and she did not want to be in this world any longer. That was the only reason she came with us to the island. She and some others came to die. That is the purpose of the beast. He prowls in the night and during the day. He is the *Grand Harvester*, the *Angel of Death*. And I can tell you one thing she wouldn't have felt a thing. I always poison them before they are eaten. I slip it in their drink or their meal. I bet she was plum happy last night dancing with the King before her peaceful end." She said stepping past Shortblade and giving him her cold shoulder.

I looked down and Hatley noticed the frown across my face. I wondered if the beast had eaten the lady while I was dancing with my King. I shuddered as I remembered his breathtaking howls and turned to hide the blush in my cheeks.

"Cheer up Lad, here have some rum. We have been through this many full moons. I think because you were younger and went to bed before nightfall, you might not remember." Hatley said as I nodded and took some of the rum he offered.

He was right.

Even last year when the ladies had come, I had gone to my room while the music started. I didn't want to be around the half-dressed ladies drunk and eventually dancing naked in the courtyard. I was there in helping burying pieces the next day. But even then, the men had spared my eyes from the full devastation by covering the bodies. I thought about these things as I drank again but this time it was O'Shady offering me some brandy.

"Tis' best not to think of such pleasantries' unappealing to thy senses. Let us be merry for we can still play music in the sun-filled courtyard and still be in good company." O'Shady said as he took his hat off and wiped the sweat from his brow.

O'Shady's hair was shoulder length and just as blonde as Shortblade's without the ribbons. It always seemed tangled but his heart was kind. I continued to garden as Cut-Throat Kathleen came over to me. She was watching me harvest more potatos and shared some rum.

The rest of the men and scantily dressed ladies came out in bliss to greet us. I really loved seeing the men happy, they deserved love. We all did. It seemed the festivities would be starting all over again as I heard a lute playing in the courtyard.

"What is this about Telulah? The boat seemed fine when I sees' her this morn. Arrrgghh." A crewman that I didn't recognize spoke out cutting everyone off.

Hatley gave him a good look and then raised his hands.

"Right then. I will tell you new recruits about Telulah and just maybe it will save your life. I will tell you the story exactly how it was told to me by me great grandfather, who had passed the story down from his great grandfather, and through the generations." Hatley said and then cleared his throat as the little butterfly sat in his beard.

"I shall tell you a story of woe arrrgghh. The Pirate King of ancient times be' in love for the first time. We met her on our voyage to some new colonies and she being the only woman we ever sailed with and the last. She was a fierce creature to be reckoned with. Her golden hair was curly and as wild as a hurricane with tied pink ribbons and she always wore her skirts unfashionably high. But to glance at her beauty was a death sentence. She was as ruthless and heartless as they come. Her being one of the only lady pirates I had ever met at that time and her name was *Telulah the Red'*. She could rob and kill you before you could blink. I never knew that women were so capable of murder until she joined us. For a woman it was unheard of to be such a good swordsman but she proved herself over and over. She was not to be trifled with. Though her looks be' that of an angel, she was more devil than human." Hatley said and drank some rum and paused for a moment looking at the Pirate King with his arms crossed in the shadows of the courtyard listening.

"Those were times of peaceful seas and happy marauding. The Great Pirate King was in love and they seemed at bliss with each new chest of treasure. We had more gold than any one of us could dream of. But we wanted more, being pirates and all. It's in our nature. I think myself would rather die than miss out on a chance for the ultimate treasure." Hatley said and took another swig of rum.

"We were on the lookout for the most glorious treasure ever beheld on earth. One drink from the Goblet of Hades would give anyone colossal strength and unseen power. The Goblet was forged out of hell and blessed by Hades himself. Hades being the ruler of the underworld had filled it with a magic potion of his blood and the taste of one drop from the cup could give a mortal the power to rule either the seas if you drank facing the North or the land if you drank facing the South. All was needed was one drop and you had the power of the God of the underworld. The map be' written in blood on the skin of some great sea monster." Hatley looked again to the Captain and raised his mug drinking a quick toast.

"But the legend never spoke of the wicked curse be' on the cup. Yes. Arrrgghh. It was never supposed to be a blessing. It was created to curse the God's and Hades' enemies. And it was never meant to make it out of the cavern, never meant be' drunk by any mere mortal." Hatley said and cleared his throat as the whole courtyard was listening intently.

"As we entered the cave of bones we knew something wasn't right but Telulah wanted the treasure. She hated the world and wanted vengeance on her enemies. It made the crew divided. There were those of us who could read the trail of twisted bones. And the bones be' truth and never lie. The ones that couldn't read the signs followed her orders blindly. I always followed the Pirate King no matter what and we went into the cave with Telulahs crew in the lead. She set off booby-traps and killed them. She being the devil; naturally she did not want to share the treasure. Except with the one she loved. I know what the Pirate King and Telulah had was fool's gold now though. She used her power of love against our King to drink from the cup facing the South and the North. At first nothing happened. She called him too weak to hold the treasure and she drank the black fluid. She drank it all facing the North. But nothing had happened or so it seemed.

So then she told the Captain she had never loved him and that she was only after the treasure. Suddenly the Captain became very ill and feverish. And that was when she stabbed him in the chest with her dagger. She took our weapons, some of the other treacherous crew, and our grand ship; leaving us stranded on this very fearsome tropical paradise named; *'The Isle of Fleshed Carnage'*.

But as her row boats were leaving, we all watched her change hideously. She transformed to the massive sea serpent never being the mortal skinned thing of beauty she once adorned. She became the ugliness her heart had always been. She always be' tyrant of a monster, but has become even more vengeful. Now her rows and rows of teeth can eat a boat in seconds and she has an unquenchable thirst for the blood of men. Her great dragon claw's grab ships and slashes into them. Instead of wings she has tentacles with many spiked horns holding the only thing human left over her giant dragon's face. And razor sharp fins cut through the water and men's hearts. *'Telulah the Red'* has been lost for decades now, but *'Telulah the Great Sea Monster'* rages in ruling the seas and seeks out the man's heart who tried to capture hers." Hatley said as he cleared his throat.

"Let this story be a warning for you. She can control the weather and create mighty storms. But in the heart of the turbulent force you think is nature is actually the great sea serpent. So much power was never meant to be held in a mortal's heart. She is after that which she can never be. And she is always after us, waiting to kill the Pirate King that still has mortal flesh on his bones." Hatley finished and you couldn't hear anyone breathing.

"If this be' true the Pirate King would be over eighty years and a magical, decrepit old fart." The new recruit Bob shouted as he laughed and the ladies laughed with him.

Then everyone roared in laughter around the courtyard.

"Oh Hatley, you have had too much drink in the hot sun." The strange new recruit laughed again and everyone started laughing.

But a few of us looked over to the Pirate King who was drinking but saw his teeth clenched.

O'Shady nudged my arm and poured brandy into my mug.

"I saw her. I saw Telulah. I was captured by the Royal Guard and in the brigs when I saw the great serpents head rise out of the water. The creature had pink ribbons attached in its tangle of horns on top its head. I barely escaped as she took a hole out of the side of the vessel the length of a sail. I was marooned on a plank of wood when Shortblade rescued me in the ocean. 'Tis true." O'Shady said and held up an ancient tattered sea mossed-ribbon that still held a light pink color.

The few of us listening turned again to see the eyes of the Pirate King which seemed to glow red in the shadows. His strong tight features of his face stole my breath away.

"But what creature be' that of the Pirate King ye say? He walks like a man yet he yield's both colossal swords like a God. He mesmerizes the ladies and casts his gargantuan sails into their devouring oceans." Hatley said loudly and we all gasped as the Pirate King suddenly appeared behind him placing his hand on Hatley's shoulder.

"I think that is enough stories for today my friend." The Pirate King said dignified as he walked away from the group and out of the courtyard of on-lookers.

Hatley nodded with an easy smile. And the crowd settled in smiles at the story.

"Dragonfly, catch us some rabbits shall ye? You catch the plumpest ones Lad. It is like you speak rabbit and they fall at your arrow." O'Shady said and passed me some more brandy.

"The rabbits love is unfortunate as I too yield my giant bow in their direction." I said and laughed as everyone laughed too.

I got to my feet and ran into the castle retrieving my long bow and arrows quickly. I heard the cheers and waved at the other fellows as they drank with their ladies and the music continued.

Making my way to the meadow seemed quicker as my heart beat faster than ever before. It felt like I was walking on clouds and floated to the meadow. Instead of getting to work, I actually laid in the sweet grass and took out of my vest pocket the rose blossom Dragon had given me. I smelt the sweetness and placed it to my lips. The rose petals were as soft as the King's red lips and just as deep in color. I stayed there and watched some clouds before actually getting to work. It was nice to just daydream here amongst the wildflowers and be at peace with the world.

It was in that moment of tranquility when I remembered dead-man's dock along the beach and shuddered at the thought of the old weathered sign that always creaked in the restless wind.

♦♦♦♦

CHAPTER 14

Today's festivities were well underway as the music played and crewmen were dancing with their partners dressed in lovely fabrics of colors bursting. Everyone seemed happy as I had brought back twice as many rabbits then yesters'eve. The bonfire was blazing but sun was still raining happiness down as the rabbits were once more skinned and impaled over the fire.

I had known my limits and was taking it lighter today as I only sipped on rum. Tonight I just wanted rest. Alas, there would be no stowing away as a lady to dance with my King. This was the last night with our visitors and the beast would be hungry with duties to perform. Everyone was even more immersed in rum than before as I stole away to the cellar to get a few more bottles of rum and a big bottle of the King's not-so-secret brandy stash. There was no sweet whispers of lovers like the night before and I hoped where ever certain people were hiding they would be happy and safe.

The King had seemed to retire earlier. The responsibilities he had were burdensome and my heart went to the tower windows which held little flames from the burning candles in each window. I don't know how he could sleep as our favorite sea shanties sang out in the night and the music seemed to blare out from inside the courtyard and all over the island.

The Pirate King would eventually be out in his best tonight and dancing with the lovely ladies. He had his duties and my mind understood that but my heart did not want to linger without his arms around me tonight.

⸎⸎⸎⸎

I don't even remember how I made my way through the jungle of vines and trees. *So much for drinking less.* I thought as I stood completely confused at my surroundings and flagrantly drunk. But here I was standing at the edge of the lagoon's warm blue-green waters. I started completely stripping off my clothes, boots and even my extra fabric. Wandering into the warm water I made two trips bringing gifts to the warm green, flat rock that Luna ruled her kingdom on. She had seen me and waved excitedly as I held up the bottles and she clapped.

One thing I had learnt about mermaids was their love for rum as much as us pirates. We laid on the rock drinking and watched the sunset across the horizon. I didn't mean to get so drunk and I don't think Luna did either as a handsome merman joined us on the rock. She had left her seashells off and I was amazed at the different reactions in her Kingdom towards me and her. It really made me wonder about the heavy value placed on nudity in our modern society. *What was the big deal? The mermaids don't hide who they are and they all coexist in beauty. Why does it have to be different for humans?* I watched as she let him steal kisses and both their skin changed to a warm orange shade that spread out from their hearts down to their fins. She shared the rum bottle with him and a deeper orange spread across his face in a blush as he passed the bottle to me. His yellow eyes almost glowed as he looked at Luna smiling warm. His long blond hair held seashells. I moved his golden hair behind his ear and he slowly touched my arm studying my tanned skin. His fingers across my arm felt like suction cups and I touched his arm that held small scales. He closed his eyes as I gently caressed his face and the orange shade of his skin grew deeper. His yellow eyes scanned me but weren't invasive. His eyes held an innocent wonder as he wiggled my toes studying them. He slowly slid his hand up my leg as I gasped. I suddenly drank more as his hands rested on my shoulders. He smiled at me warmly and I was still in shock but smiled. Suddenly he reached into the water and gifted a necklace of shimmering small seashells to me.

He turned and grabbed Luna in his arms kissing her deeply as his tail swished over hers. Luna smiled over to me as he licked her neck. I heard her say the word; "Ulik" and pointed to him as he continued to kiss her down her body and I blushed as she sang high.

When Luna was drunk she would sing. Under normal circumstances her voice was like heaven itself, captivating and otherworldly. But when she was drunk she was so off key and loud that it was easy to see why no one came here, other than the fear of being eaten. But I loved listening to her and watching her now orange skin shimmer in the pinks of the fading sunlight. I liked how she accepted me for who I was, even without a tail. She sang in this language of love from the universe that amazed me. Ulik laid on his back with his hands under his head just now with a huge grin and closed his eyes listening to Luna sing.

I sat beside Ulik just as happy in listening to her higher off-key notes. *This is the life I thought as I looked at Ulik at peace with the world and it was exactly how I felt.*

Suddenly she reached over and touched the Jolly Roger scar on my forearm. The raised seared flesh was where the Royal Guard had marked us with the symbol of the pirate and our flag. All of us had it including the Pirate King and I knew the next time we were caught we would hang. Luna frowned as she felt the rough angry skin and I just smiled and shrugged.

"Tis' the life I willingly choose my dear friend. At least if I perish it will be with my blood brethren." I said and smiled.

Her smile was vague but seemed to understand as she nodded and then she continued to sing but now softly in her ancient language.

All three of us continued to drink heavily and finished one bottle off easily. I loved nights like this as we listened to the howling and passed out on the rock beside each other. Ulik was on his back and stretched his arms open like pillows for us; as I placed my head on his arm. His wide smile was peaceful as he snored and I placed my head on his chest as Luna placed her head on his other side. I reached my hand across his scaled skin to hold Luna as she mirrored me and both drifted to sleep.

※※※※

In the middle of the night, I half-awoke to loving whispers. Somehow we had changed positions and I was on my back as Ulik draped his tail across me like a shield. Luna had always done that when we slept on the rock. But it was sweet that they both held me like some treasure and I adored being surrounded by their affections as I fell asleep in harmony.

※※※※

That night I dreamt of being carefully taken off the rock away from the sleeping sirens. The Pirate King was whispering to me in some ancient language and forbidden kisses. And I happily indulged in. We were laying now in the meadow on the softest grass surrounded by all the wildflowers. His sensual skin trembled as we moved more vigorously worshipping each other's bodies with tender kisses. And in the moonlight's secret sleep finally overcame my senses, feeling safe in his strong loving arms.

🌱🌱🌱

I awoke again with his arms and legs wrapped like a blanket around me. His golden earring was pink from the hues of the sunrise. We were on the beach by the ocean and I could hear the waves breaking against the rocks. We were so close to the water I could feel the surf spray over my legs. My head ached as I snuggled into his fragrant chest full of lavender and sea moss. His arms were around me snug as we lay there in pure content.

But my eyes went wide in surprise matching his startled blue eyes at this heavenly discovery of waking just before dawn.

"Poesia, last night was the last time I could be seduced by your lovely charms. We have to get up. We cannot be caught. I feel I have lost my head in my desire for you." His deep voice held a faint panic.

"Okay Dragon." I said and put my leg around him.

"My lovely we have to…" His deep voice was shaking as with his needful desire that I tilted my hips into forbiddenly.

He lovingly rolled me to my back as we kissed indulging in the desires of our hearts that needed to be fulfilled. He surrendered and then collapsed on to me; happily dead to the world.

"Oh my beauty, my sweet divine; we need to move from this

forbidden heaven. Now that was the last time of this forbidden romance in the sunlight." Dragon said as his chest deeply raised and fell.

"Yes Sir." I said dreamily as he stayed lying on top of me listening to my wildly beating heart.

Slowly he sat up and I with him, as I clutched my head.

"The rum. We need more rum or brandy." I said as I rubbed my head.

"No I think that is what keeps getting us into these wonderful situations of temptation and fulfilling our deepest desires. We need to get dressed." He said as his deep voice sighed after.

"Yes Sir." I said more drearily as I looked at his sultry mouth with blood all over his chin and body.

It was the first time I really looked at him from our dream-like, love-making craze; and I gasped. His hands and feet were caked with blood and mud. I noticed my hands were bloody and full of mud too. Then I saw the thin golden chain with the golden band hanging between my chest and under the seashell necklace. He worth a matching ring necklace and I gasped.

"My King we must have..." I said as I realized we weren't in the lagoon anymore; we were in the open on the beach shore surrounded by dead pieces of rabbits. The fur and guts were everywhere including our naked bodies.

"Let's get to the water and clean up. And then we'll find our clothes." His deep voice was still shaking as he grabbed my hand and gently pulled me to the water.

I couldn't help but giggle as we gingerly washed each other off completely and he sweetly kissed me in the salty water that turned a dark crimson.

"I think last night is coming back to me. I think I remember where our clothes are. I remember going to the hidden cave of bones. It's the beast's lair." I said as my voice was shaking.

"The brandy has brought our deepest desires to the surface and cannot be revoked. What else do you remember?" He said sadly as his eyes looked worriedly into mine.

I remembered bits and pieces and then looked at the five-pointed star on his left hand. And he took my left hand that held the same five-pointed star. He placed our hands together and I hugged him tight.

"I remember going into the cave and giving myself to the beast. I coaxed you into transforming into human and you did. And then we hunted for rabbits together and I caught a huge one with my bare hands. And then we made love in this forbidden cave in a magical marriage ritual of blood."

"So you know this is forever. What was done in the shadows cannot be revoked. You know the legend is real and that is why we dock here each month before the full of the moon. You know I am cursed. And I have chosen you as my willing bride, my mate for eternity." His gruffy voice stirred my soul.

He had sat with his hands covering his face and I moved his hands over my heart as I sat on his lap. I placed my loving arms over his shoulder and gazed in his dreamy blue eyes. As I held him, he moved some sand off my face and we paused in looking in each other's eyes.

"Now that you know, you can never leave me. It would rip the only bit of human heart left in my dark soul." He whispered.

"Who says I want to ever leave you my husband and my King." I said as I kissed him and he sweetly kissed me back holding me tightly.

Each kiss was full of adoration. I lay my head over his shoulder and could feel his heavy beating heart full of a bursting enrapture.

"You are mine forever Poesia. I cannot be free of you now. It would surely kill my immortal heart." He confessed softly as I felt his fangs bite into my neck with his kiss.

"In your arms is the only place I want to be Dragon." I whispered back as he drank from me into an ultimate shared euphoric state.

It was an unexplained need from being together and secretly loving each other for so long. My soft moans in his ear and mouth were caught in his breath stealing kisses.

As the sun peaked through the ocean's rippling ceiling, our love reminded me of the flowing water. Where there was no beginning and no end with such a fluid dominion having no space between our souls joining in some forbidden magic of lost souls finding each other.

He slowly stood up carrying me and then helping me to my feet. Gently he leaned down and kissed my neck breathing this warmth of healing. We walked on the wet sand to the ocean holding hands and then running in feeling free in the rush of the waves. We swam in the magic of the dawn with the pink streams of light through the deep blue. Going deeper; we swam further down to the hidden collapsed entrance of the cave of bones and the mighty beast's lair.

A flash of a memory came to my mind of us making love on a stone table, where he had professed his love for me, for all of eternity. We had shared an intimate moment of drinking from an emerald encrusted goblet some deep crimson drink. In the heat of the moment of climax he had taken a diamond clad silver dagger slicing our left hands and then holding them together in a sacred ritual of marriage and commitment between us. Vowing to love me even in death he burst through my soul in octaves so deep I thought he could feel my heart vibrating off his echo. He healed our hands and a five-pointed star was now engraved forever on my left hand; that matched his left hand.

I focused on this morning though and seen the pillars coming into view as he pulled my hand in getting me to the underwater opening.

Three giant spiraling pillars and grand flat jade steps leading from the ocean into the palace was even grander with golden designs etched an ancient language all over the pillars. With a wave of his hand a magic lit up the torches along the wall.

"Last night you found me here. No one had ever dared to come into this place of my forgotten palace. You are the first mortal to have searched me out and found my hidden sanctuary." He said in his deep voice which seemed to seduce me where I stood in awe of the two thrones and the two golden crowns upon them.

"In fact no creature has been in my real throne room and seen my true form in all my glory and lived." He said as he turned from me and looked over to the thirty-three-foot tall statue made of some onyx like polished texture.

While he spoke I was lost in the magnificence of this massive room that held the same ancient writings in red paint written vertically on the walls and ceiling surfaces. There was a giant tapestry behind the intricately carved thrones of a wolf-like man with a golden crown holding what appeared to be a pomegranate and offering it to a crowned woman in the moon. As I looked more closely I realized it wasn't a pomegranate but a heart in the lycanthropes clawed hands. A chill ran down my spine as I caught his eyes now red watching me.

The gigantic statue was of the same crowned lycanthrope holding a colossal ruby in the shape of a heart up to the ceiling. In admiration I walked over to the statue and placed my hands on the clawed man-like feet. The towering statue was slightly different though as the wolf's mouth was open and its fangs were elongated. It held massive carved wings attached to its back. They were carved so detailed it was like the statue could take flight. I reached my hands up to touch the magnificent feathers and suddenly he reached for my hands.

"Last night you came to me and I could not give up my love for you. It has been growing deep inside my lonely soul since I first found you dying. My love has increased from taking care of you and toughening you up for the cruel world. To now, changing these last years to becoming your protector and your forbidden admiration for me had been driving my senses wild. And I have fought with my darkness this last year to not read your mind and to not listen to my heart. But these last nights on the island with you have changed that completely. I cannot go back to wanting kisses from you. I need to feel your lips, your touch against my bare coursing skin. I need to feel that fire of your chosen adoration for me." His said and cleared his throat.

"But our love was forbidden. I am your King and should not want you. I confirmed what beat in my heart for you was real when you first kissed my lips. I don't know what has become of my royal senses. But your eyes hold this deep love for me that I could not escape even if I wanted to. I am immortal and have tried to stay away from loving you but you have slain me. I am forever yours. I place my fragile heart in your hands Poesia. Do not hurt me like my past. I could not bare it." His deep voice was full of sorrow as he turned from me.

Yet I grabbed his hand holding it to my heart once more. My heart had been thumping through my chest wildly and it was so strong I needed him to feel my love.

"Oh Dragon, I have always loved you. But since these last years I couldn't deny the strong feelings I have for you. But what is time but a droplet in the ocean of life. I give thee my hand like I did last night and promise my undying love for all eternity; my dear loving King and ruler of my soul's heart." I said in a huskier voice than normal in my mortal confession that never wavered.

He held my hands and gazed into my eyes with only the galaxies and stars through his. He was looking at me like I was everything he had ever dreamed of and I knew this because I was looking at him the same way. He picked me up and carried me back over to the tomb that held our blood from the night before and laid me down; quickly covering me in passionate kisses. I could feel the power between us as his long hair swept across me and he indulged in my sweetness. We cried out in our explosion of volcanic fireworks and ethereal heights of love. And like lava we melted into each other. I was positive no mere mortal has ever seen this love before as I looked at the ceiling and saw the stars moving in a swirl of cosmic driven affection. Sweetly his soft kisses fluttered over my skin.

"I love you my dear Poesia. You are mine forever now my Queen; my mate for life." His voice out of breath hauntingly whispered in my ear.

"Yes, my King." I whispered back as he slowly made me shriek for joy.

All my life I had hated men for what they had done to me, except with him. I freely opened my heart and soul to his.

On the streets of London there had been a dangerous drug of illusions that people referred to as chasing the dragon before they died. In this moment, I felt like I was chasing my own dragon as I called his name and my body enraptured to his sweet motion of rhythm. He turned me again so I could lie on his chest now and held me tight as he kissed my head.

"Oh my sweet Poesia, will you promise to still love me tomorrow and for all eternity?" His deep voice whispered to my heart.

"I promise to love you only until forever, my King." I said and then kissed him long and true of all the affection in my being.

"We have to be safe my Queen. I have many enemies." He said and held his left arm around me showing our matching painful tattoos from the Royal Guard.

Then he opened his left palm beside mine showing our matching star symbols and interlocked our fingers as he kissed me.

"Some of my enemies are known and some unknown. Trust my heart is only yours forever more, even as we keep up appearances for a short spell." He whispered and then slowly brushed his thumb against my lips and then kissed me ever so sweetly.

"Anything for you Dragon." I whispered and kissed his chest as I squeezed him in our embrace.

"Our bond is forever my sweet Queen." He whispered as he kissed the tattoo star on my hand once more and my ring.

In one blink of an eye I was looking into the oceans of his enchanting blue eyes happier and more in love than I could ever think mortally possible. But then he snapped his fingers and our clothes magically appeared on the throne as he helped me over to dress. He started wrapping my chest and midriff kissing me gingerly as we dressed.

I glanced over to our stone bed and noticed the stone slab read 1414 A.D. and carved into the rock was a sleeping crowned knight resting with his sword and shield across his armor. It appeared to be some ancient casket.

"If ever you want to know my past, just say the words and I shall tell you. But know you are my future." At the sound of his voice it seduced my being and I looked up into his devoted blue eyes that were as soft as clouds.

I didn't care about his past. He is mysterious and supernatural. *Maybe he is of darkness and magic. But he is everything I have ever wanted. Even if his soul is damned for all of eternity, as well as my own for being in love with him; I don't care. How could such a loving guardian and magical creature be considered evil? It makes me wonder tis' like the necessary parts of life. Death is inevitable for everyone. And it doesn't matter if you are good or evil in life. Maybe he is of the same magic as death?* I thought as I was lost in his beauty.

"Hush your thoughts my Pet. Just know my undead heart beats for nothing less than infinity for yours." He said as he took my hand and placed it over his fiercely beating heart.

"Undead? But your heart beats faster than a raven's wings and I have seen your breath in the chill of the morning." I said as I gazed into his bewitching blue eyes.

"Tis' mere muscle memory and has been dead for a very long time. Tis' not out of necessity my love." He whispered softly as he placed a kiss behind my ear.

I sighed heavenly and hugged him. We moved to a vine entangled stair case that spiraled to the ceiling. He took my hand and gently led me the way snapping his fingers as the torches blew out. When he opened the heavy door; I realized it was an obscured door cut out of the massive weeping willow by the lagoon. The bones of wind chimes swayed together making an eerie song of sadness. As he closed the door firm you could not even see the seams in the tree's bark. It was completely hidden in broad sight.

"Here is where I shall leave you my Queen. But know wherever I am, my heart only beats for yours. We must remain secret until I discover our enemy amongst us, my love. Be brave my Queen until night fall when we can be together again." His deep scruffy voice lifted on the last sentence as he wickedly smiled and placed wet kisses on my hand.

"Yes my King." I answered so smitten I hoped he felt the warmth in my eyes and I kissed his hand back.

Then his long strides swept him away as I lingered in the silence of the lagoon and the early morning clouds of my absent heart.

⁂

CHAPTER 15

I left my boots in the multicolored sand and ran into the slightly chilly blue-green waters. Easily I glided to Luna's rock leaving my clothes on the shore along with my lovesick heart I needed to abandon. I knew the ladies and Cut-Throat Kathleen would be leaving today. And they would be departing with less people than had voyaged here with their affections.

Suddenly Luna and Ulik appeared on the rock and they gave me a warm embrace. Her hair was light green and far lighter than the seaweed surrounding the rock. And her lips were bluer than a sapphire's sparkle in the sun. She was too beautiful and magnetic for words. *To always be so free. How wonderful that would be.* I thought as I sat there while she pulled something familiar out of the water.

"Oh Luna you saved it." I said excitedly in looking at the exquisite bottle of rum she had preserved.

She smiled and Ulik uncorked it giving me the first drink and then she drank. *This morning is surely the loveliest of mornings.* I thought as I felt exhausted from last night. Luna was positioning herself for a good nap on the rock, like she always did when she suntanned and it seemed like the right minute to catch a catnap in. Ulik extended his arms as pillows for us and I went back to my napping position with them. I wouldn't be needed for a bit yet and decided to go back to sleep. *What a glorious life and lovely nap friends.* I thought as I extended my hand to Luna's and she grabbed it holding it to her lips. Then she noticed the ring on my new necklace and smiled warmly at me before closing her yellow eyes.

🌾🌾🌾🌾

I awoke quickly to the sound of high-pitch laughter from a melodic voice and agitated splashing. As I wiped the sleet out of my eyes I saw Shortblade with a bottle of rum, flagrantly naked and raving drunk making his way into the shallows of the lagoon. His speech was gibberish and his slow staggered movements toward us were appalling as Luna continued to laugh as she pointed. Ulik's face looked frightened at the splashing sounds getting louder. I felt his long tale covering my lower region as I stretched and sat up still sleepy.

"You laugh now but once I get my hands on you temptress, you will be sorry and next I will kill the beast with my bare hands. And I will be rid of all your magical nonsense." Shortblade shouted as his blonde hair flowed across his muscular chest.

Then I saw what Luna was laughing at as she pointed and though it be' wrong I started laughing too. We both giggled and I finally realized why the men had named our new crewmate; *'Shortblade'.* He had been blessed in looks but the feather in the Captain's hat had more girth and length than Shortblade's impotence in the frigid water.

Shortblade's face looked more sinister as soon as he seen me stretch and then laugh with Luna. Now his face resembled a ripe tomato out of the garden. His eyes went wide as he looked at me sitting on the rock. Ulik immediately moved his long tail over my lap fanning his fins and then he moved his body like a shield in front of mine so Shortblade wouldn't see any more than he already had.

Luna continued to be fearless in her high pitch laughter with her ebony shell crown adorning her perfect head of flowing, curled green hair. Her antennas were always on alert but shook with her laughter. She hadn't even stopped to put her seashells on as she taunted him by shaking her very oversized breasts in his direction. But I knew what she was doing and I took her arm. She looked at me with a quizzical brow. I shook my head 'no' and she instantly pouted. Her yellow eyes were suddenly sad as she bared her razor teeth and in defiance gave a high-pitch scream at him.

"Woah." Shortblade said and seemed to sober him up as he ran back out of the lagoon stopping to grab his clothes. Luna laughed even louder and pointed at his frozen-lack-of-enthusiasm as he ran. I watched as his angry eyes burned into mine, not in hers.

"Luna you can't eat him. He may not be nice but he's my shipmate." I said as I placed my hand on her cheek.

She smiled and nodded not making a sound. I smiled too and nodded at Shortblade's cold-water, morning misfortune. I bet she ruined his giant ego but that was better than what she was really going to do to him. She was tempting him to his doom and he hadn't even realized it. If he would have been any closer even I couldn't have saved him from her hunger to devour his flesh. Her kingdom had become accustomed to eating a particular man's organ. In fact, in the siren culture it was some fancy dessert. I knew this from over the years of stumbling in on her feasts.

"I have to go Luna. I will try and see you before we ship off." I said and kissed her cheek and Ulik's.

They both smiled and embraced me in a quick goodbye. I jumped off the rock and glided to the shore. Shortblade had grabbed my boots when he got spooked. It didn't matter though I was used to running barefoot all over this tropical island. I dressed quickly and started running to the castle. As I ran to the courtyard I heard roars of laughter and came upon a very red-faced man still trembling naked as he clumsily dressed. Shortblade was trying to warn the men of the mermaids but they were teasing him about running naked through the island.

"I guess mermaids don't want cold sausage, eh Shortblade? They only want hot oversized bratwurst. Tis' chilly this morn, ain't it?" Hatley said as he laughed so hard his belly shook.

I started to laugh because Hatley's laughter was contagious and Shortblade gave me a murderous look. The same look was in the Royal Guards eyes as they started carving the Pirate King's initial into my skin to get me to speak. I gave them nothing though. The code was what I lived for and it was death before dishonor and betrayal. I grinned over to Shortblade because I knew his death was in the lagoon and he had been spared.

"No harm has done Shortblade. It's good those sinister sirens didn't want you. If they did fancy your giant sword you wouldn't be alive for us to even mock your cold little tadpole." Hatley said and laughed again but stopped as he noticed the evil looks Shortblade was giving me.

"There has to be something with Dragonfly. He laughs with the mermaids he swims and naps with." Shortblade had a smug smile as I knew what he was trying to do to me in front of all the men.

"That's because the lad seduced their Queen with his massive sausage. Didn't you Dragonfly?" Hatley said more jolly but his eyes squinted to Shortblade.

"Yes. That's right. She loves me and I love her." I spoke up and laughed with my crews rolling laughter.

As Shortblade fumbled with his pants; the ladies had start to come out into the courtyard giggling as he was growing desirably hard from being heated with anger. His gaze tried to burn holes into my green eyes that never flinched. But I sure did smile as the laughter continued and I smiled at the free show he was giving the ladies. Their scandalous eyes eat him up and I knew I couldn't break gaze as his eyes challenged mine. But my cheeks grew rosy just like the giggling hens when he accidently dropped his pants again and had a rock hard time of taming his minotaur back into his pants. I heard sorrows from the ladies as he tied the string hastily. Suddenly he stole O'Shady's dagger and ran to me giving me a warning slice across my arm as he pointed the tip at my chest.

"Prove it Dragonfly. Let me see this massive sausage of yours in front of everyone. In fact, we can compare right now. Now that my sobriety has awakened my proud flesh; I can guarantee I am more expansive sober and warm than you will ever be." Shortblade whispered and prodded the sharp tip deeper making a spot of blood come through my white shirt.

But I smiled at his growing arrogance and drank some rum that someone had passed me even as his sword stilled. *I am way too drunk for this nonsense Shortblade. You have to take a joke. Everyone always teased me about my small tadpole before you. Besides, even if you slay me right now; I know I will be avenged.* I thought but continued to smile and drink rum. My arm was bleeding as well as my shirt but everything seemed happy in the sun with rum.

Shortblade dropped the dagger and instead held me up against the wall by the cuff of my shirt. He stole the rum as I yawned and the men laughed.

"I will get you Dragonfly. Why should you get to be happy?"

Shortblade whispered into my ear just as Hatley had pulled his sword quietly to Shortblade's back.

Shortblade suddenly threw the bottle of rum against the wall and re-adjusted his grip back on my shirt collar. But just as the glass broke the Pirate King appeared and suddenly everyone stilled including me.

"Men we ship out in the wake of morning next. Sober up but pack many cases of rum for our voyage." His deep menacing voice rang out in the courtyard but was like the happiest melody in my ears.

"Aye Aye Captain." We all said harmoniously.

The crew all immediately smiled as wide as our sails would be flying in catching the ocean air. *I love our ship. There is something barbaric about Telulahs Revenge and her burnt wooden planks that seemed older than the flat earth. She travels at supernatural speeds when needed. And I suspect the Captain's magic is at the helm.* I thought as I ignored the precarious situation I was in. The Pirate King immediately gave Shortblade a ferocious look that made him free me and back away from me.

"Shortblade you'd be smart to stay away from those tricksters in the lagoon. As sweet as they be' to them your flesh is sweeter. I'm sure it is Dragonfly's youthful looks tis' the only thing that has saved his skin from parting his bones. Don't be foolish as to think you'd be' of that kind of fairy magic; even in being of bulky breadth and beautiful." Hatley grimly said now even closer to me with his sword ready to strike Shortblade.

"Shortblade let me remind you, the bones hanging from the giant weeping willow overlooking the lagoon was not decorated by us." The Pirate King's deep voice and haunting blue eyes made Shortblade tremble as he backed against the wall.

My happiness faded in mentioning the great weeping willow overlooking the lagoon. It wasn't something I looked upon even in daily passings. I had actually forgotten the partially mummified corpses and bones that swayed in the breeze making an unspeakable wind chime from the dead. *I wonder how many men the mermaids have actually eaten?* I shuddered at that thought.

"I'm going to kill those mermaids. I'm going to kill all the magical creatures on the island. I'm ready for the bravery test Captain, tonight in fact." Shortblade's voice stammered but he put out his hand to shake on the deal.

"You seek valor and honor but I hope it will not be your grave you find tonight." The Pirate King's voice changed deeper and I watched Shortblade tremble as they shook hands.

"I am willing to risk it all, my King. Whatever shall be, I will honor thee." Shortblade said as the Pirate King's hand glowed in his.

"Fine it be' a deal. When the moon is high the hunt will start. No one will aide you as is the tradition. The beast will find you and either you shall live or die. But first you need to finish burying the bodies from last night. Everyone else dismissed." The Pirate King's deep voice boomed through the courtyard.

"Yes Sir. I only have two left and body parts from last night which I shall finish burying immediately." Shortblade said as his breathing went rapid.

"Excuse me Sir." Shortblade turned and puked by the wall away from me, the Pirate King and Hatley.

"Dragonfly, I need my coffee brought to my quarters. You can get yourself cleaned up afterwards and then help Shortblade." The Pirate King's deep voice was menacing and I nodded as I walked to the rose bush grabbing one and stuffing it under my hat in the courtyard.

I grabbed another bountiful rose and handed it to Cut-Throat Kathleen who had been watching all the commotion and had her musket pointed on Shortblade in the shadows. She lowered her weapon and actually set it by the door to smell the sweetness of the rose and then gave me a huge bear hug without saying a word. She then strolled towards the Pirate King.

"Yes, my servant Philip needs a good grave as he was a good man." Cut-Throat Kathleen spoke with her chin high and dignified.

"Philip? Oh no." I whispered as I stood by the kitchen.

"He confessed to me he was in love with someone he could never be with because of his status. He said that he was delaying the inevitable and needed a quick death to numb the pain in his heart from seeing his true love with others." Cut-Throat Kathleen said sincerely and a little tear came out of her eye.

I went into the castle kitchen door and seen Shortblade taking some water and washing his face but I was the only one that seen his tears that followed.

"Shortblade I am so sorry. I never knew." I whispered as I grabbed his arm and he turned to face me as he frantically wiped the tears flowing.

"I didn't either. So spare me your sympathies. Now excuse me while I go bury my best friend." Shortblade whispered as he held my hand but gently removed it and left me abruptly alone in the kitchen.

My heart went out for my troubled adversary. Even with our quarrel he didn't deserve to have his love lost to him. I made the Captain's coffee but my legs seemed to drag in my steps up to the towers room as my heart wept for lost love. I went through the door and into the wanting arms waiting for me. This pleasant surprise uplifted my soul.

"Okay let's check your arm that Shortblade has made a mess of and we shall see the other wound." The Pirate King started unbuttoning my vest and shirt as he made me sit in his chair.

Then he parted the wrapped fabric making sure I hadn't been stabbed deep.

"Glad tis' only a scratch and he didn't hurt your magnificent breasts." The Pirate King said as he held and kissed each through the fabric wrapping.

"What is the matter my dear Queen?" His deep voice was full of concern.

"It's Shortblade, he is utterly devastated. I think he wanted the mermaids to eat him this morning." I said as he tried to kiss my sadness away.

"Yes I know he was shocked to find Philip with the bodies to be buried. It hurt him a great deal but he excused himself. That is why only he has the task today as the others escort the ladies to their waiting boats by dead-man's dock. And since he feels closest to you than any other shipmate; you need to extend your hand in friendship." He said as he healed the scratch on my arm and chest.

Suddenly I heard a growl as he snapped his fingers and we were holding each other in his bed. My clothes were now bloodless and across his chair along with his. And I was wrapped in his loving arms.

"Let us not think of unpleasant things my sweet as we steal this prohibited scorching love consuming me." He whispered into my hair and then inhaled me heavily.

"A forbidden flame of your love is what I live for my King." I said and giggled.

He started caressing my face with kisses becoming more avidly with his colossal contentment for me. *I'm so in trouble and so in heavenly love.*

"Yes, you are." He answered my thoughts as his fangs grew with his smile.

🌿🌿🌿🌿

CHAPTER 16

In another section of the forest the sun never shined and the sweet song of the birds couldn't be heard. It was as if God wept continuously in this obscure and gloomy place that seemed to always have a hovering light mist. You could see the mysterious rainbow through the falls over yonder but it was always out of reach in this crypt of a shadowy garden of gravestones.

The stone markings were ancient in other languages giving a creepy foreboding. One of the unnerving monuments was by far the massive stone slab marked *'Telulah'*. Which I dreaded to even think of what piece of the sea monster was buried there.

But many of the tombstones held carvings of just detailed pictures. Those were moss covered graves that held only body portions of men and women alike in a warped collection of entrails and feet. It always surprised me how the beast had a particular flavor it couldn't get enough of, just like the mermaids. And we all knew this from what was left of the bodies we buried each month.

Most of the gore the crew had spared me from but that was not the case today. Waiting behind a tree, I eavesdropped on Shortblade having what seemed like a fight with himself; as he threw pieces of body parts into the first grave and started filling it with dirt.

But he had propped Philip's intact body beside the next tombstone. I shouldn't say intact. Philip was missing his heart which was clearly ripped out of his chest. Philip's face was frozen in a heartbreak of sadness and his opened hand was rigid in a fatal offered gesture. I could hear Shortblade's angry voice yelling and watched as he moved earth with his heavy spade.

"Philip you knew I loved you. I was going to give you my castle once I stole it back from the wretched Evil King Vermin. You already had my heart. Wasn't I enough for you?" Shortblade's severity in his voice matched his actions as he turned around and punched Philip's hard sorrowful face.

"I hate you. You know I always hated you. You were right." He yelled as he continued to fill the pit.

"You were one droplet in an ocean of millions of lovers that I had at my beck and call. You were nothing but a lowly bastard. And I don't care that you offered your life to the beast over my love. I would rather it this way." He turned to yell at Philip's corpse sitting beside him.

"You know what? I thank heavens I don't have to look at your ugly poverty stricken self ever again." Shortblade yelled at the corpse and punched him in the opened chest again and again.

"I will bury our empty promises in millions of lover's. I will love so openly that I hope it burns you in hell. And I hope you see each touch and caress of the love you will never feel again. I curse you Philip. I HATE YOU." He screamed as he punched Philip's opened chest until it collapsed.

But Philip's body didn't fight back. Philip's sad face didn't change to anger. Philip didn't scream back. He couldn't hold Shortblade as he cried out in the darkness. Philip's tearless eyes still held the same sorrowfulness and his hand still opened in offer to the unknown.

Suddenly Shortblade threw Philips body wrathfully into the last open grave. The headstone of which had a nameless carved heart on it.

"I hate you Philip. I HATE YOU." He screamed at the top of his lungs and started filling the pit up with dirt.

Then Shortblade dropped to his knees and screamed again in wretched agony at the top of his lungs. He clutched his chest and screamed as he started moaning Philips name. He was wailing uncontrollably in the anguish and his whole body shook. He jumped into the pit suddenly and dragged Philip back out of the grave. He sat there hugging Philip's corpse and kissing the blue face over and over.

"I'm sorry my love. I'm sorry. I love you. Why did you do this to us? We were supposed to be together for all time. My darling. My beautiful Philip. You promised me. You promised me." He wailed as he rocked back and forth holding Philip tightly.

"God I need you. What am I supposed to do now you are gone? My sweet. My best friend. My only love." He cried out.

He continued to rock back and forth holding Philip tighter and caressing him.

"What am I supposed to do? You left me with nothing." He sobbed out into the darkness.

"I love you my sweet and I will love you for all time. In my heart you'll have to stay as I go through this empty life alone. God I love you." He spoke as he wept on Philip's mud covered shoulder.

He was crying softly into Philips shoulder. Rocking them in a tight embrace and just clinging to the motionless body longer. He lingered in holding his beloved and it seemed hours went by with his endless tears.

He cleared his throat loudly and wiped his face on his sleeve rolling them immediately back up. Clearing his throat again he stood up with his hands on his hips and paused to look at Philip.

"I love you my dear best friend. Though we shall never speak again the memory of you I shall hold in my soul forever. Goodbye my love." His voice full of sadness as he kissed Philip's blue cheek one last time.

Then I watched as he gently lowered his body into the open grave carrying Philips corpse very carefully. As he got out I could hear him still sobbing as he slowly placed a little muddy dirt in the pit.

My hand waivered over my heart and my tears silently flowed down my cheeks for him but I was unable to go over and comfort him. I stayed hidden around the purple hibiscus tree that seemed to be rotting with the surrounding melancholy.

I didn't have the words as my heart broke in hearing his sorrow but I couldn't watch him be alone and disheartened anymore, so I stepped on a branch purposefully ending the silence of the forest around him.

CHAPTER 17

I cleared my throat and stepped out of the shadows as Shortblade stood with his hand on the top of the gravestone. He looked away as he wiped his face vehemently and his nose on his muddy shirt. He grabbed his shovel and added more dirt very slowly over Philip's grave.

Without words I offered him the flask I had taken up to carrying and I grabbed the other shovel.

"Gentle with the dirt please." Shortblade snapped but there was a gentile way about his grasp of the flask and his slow drink.

He made a sour face immediately afterwards.

"Uuugghh brandy. Where in the hell did you get this God awful stuff Dragonfly?" He said and took another drink.

"I will place the dirt in only loving piles Shortblade. I promise." I said and placed my hand over my heart.

"I am grateful you are here and not another crewmate. I wouldn't want them to think I am weak." He said again as he frantically wiped tears and drank more.

"It's okay Shortblade. I understand." I said as I patted his back.

"You don't. You have never lost your best friend." He said as he couldn't wipe the tears flowing and didn't hide it.

"That is where you are wrong. I had a best friend and she died in my arms in the orphanage before I ran away. I keep her memory down somewhere in my heart. I remember not being able to carry the burden of missing her so much. And then I was beaten nearly to death and felt the Dark Angel's embrace. It was like I could reach up and grasp Norah's hand in the clouds, but I was brought back to life." I said and shuddered at that thought while he gazed over to me.

"Since my new life I have found friendships even stronger than before. Do not give up my friend. Your day in the sun can still be had." I said as I continued to shovel and he grabbed my arm suddenly.

He took me in a huge hug just then and I hugged him back as he cried on my shoulder.

"I thought I was the only one." Shortblade said as he cleared his throat and straightened himself up.

"We are all connected in sorrows. The life of a pirate is magnificent and filled with a despair unmentionable. We were not meant for having society's blessings. Did you know Hatley used to be a nobleman and a general in a great army? He had taken a wife and they had children when a great war broke out between the kingdoms. He defended his lands while they burned his castle to the ground with everyone he loved inside. The castled still burned when the Pirate King found him and rescued him." I said and cleared my throat.

"All of us have experienced this heartache. It doesn't make it easier but we have each other to lean on. We are thicker than thieves and our blood and bond is stronger than any place that society has to offer.

Remember as you go hunt the beast tonight that we are all with you. You are on this island with the Pirate King's blessing and we all share the same mark. You have never been alone since the moment you saved us from the Royal Guard and the Pirate King saved you back." I said as I rolled up my sleeves showing off the scratch he gave me earlier but my mark stood out on my left forearm.

Shortblade's sleeves had been rolled up and he looked at the same skull and cross bones in his raised flesh on his left arm for a moment and then wiped his face once more. He drank than passed me the flask and gave me a warm smile before making the sour face. I smiled back and took a big swig from the flask making the worst sour face imagined. I had gulped and hiccupped after.

"Why brandy? Dragonfly this stuff could grow the much needed hair on your chest." He laughed as he took another drink making the sour face as he passed it back.

"It gets you drunk quicker and it is quite dangerous in making you forget." I said and smiled as I took more immediately wiping the smile off my face.

We finished shoveling in silence and Shortblade picked some flowers that seemed brighter than the gloom as I sneezed.

"Let's go to the meadow and watch the pretty ladies leave." I said and laughed.

"Oh my dear Dragonfly, we both know that a ladies' company is not what us oddities are after. But yes I would like to get the hell out of this blasted rain." He said and laughed.

He stopped to kiss the gravestone before he left with me through the forest. We left the shovels in this rotting place as they were always needed. He moved branches so I could easily walk with him like two friends and it was the first time he wasn't in competition with me. He wasn't trying to one-up me. We stumbled a little out to the very edge of the field that gave way to endless white sands and the ocean far below.

We sat in the sunshine of the meadow surrounded by the wildflowers and watched the ocean. The groups of ladies and men were being escorted delicately to dead-man's dock. We could see the ladies extravagantly leaving in scantily clad dresses with their little parasails twirling in the sunbeams and some were kissing sailors before they got on the little row boats.

But my eye caught the ancient gigantic sign that was hung in plain sight beside dead-man's dock. The sign had been there since before I became a pirate and the tree it hung off was older than time itself. The sign was nailed to a prehistoric tree whose fingered branches and leaves stretched across the sky. And some wayward branches were downwards almost feeling the ocean.

From my vantage point you could clearly see the weather-beaten twisted rot of the wood which held something more gruesome than any made up fairytale. The ancient sign had a gargantuan withered monster clawed fin nailed to it. On the gangly clawed-like-finger lay a golden wedding ring embedded in the scales and it glinted in the sunlight.

Every time I looked at this sign it gave me shivers down my spine. It was too harsh a reality of the sea monster that was very real and ready to eat and destroy our ship every single time we sailed.

The warning sign was written in a dark stained crimson color and only had three words but those three words struck fear in everyone who read them.

The sign read; "Beware of Telulah."

CHAPTER 18

We all sat in the courtyard where the ceremony began at dusk. Now that the ladies had gone the men had settled back to normalness having gotten all their feisty energy out of their systems. Hatley passed me a mug and I clanged my mug with his right away. We all had war paint on our faces from the ash of bonfires past as we sat around this huge campfire.

The drums boomed in the night as our glorious Captain and Pirate King stepped out in his decorated gold buttoned vest and fancy plumped cotton shirt. His black hat with an undeniable crease worn dashing was adorned with exotic and rare orange peacock feathers. His eerie pale blue eyes were striking and looked like they had dream travelled through a million full moons. And his dark-tanned skin glowed in a honey sweetness of being kissed by a million suns. He was handsomely bewitching and hauntingly dangerous but we all adored our fearsome leader.

The rushed chanting and drums stopped as he raised his hand to speak.

"My fellow pirates tonight we induct our fellow crewmate; Robert 'Shortblade' Edwardian Nobly into our bravery test of honor. The rules are simple, out best the beast and stay alive after the crack of daylight. If you are worthy the beast shall not kill thee and you will whole heartedly join our blood pack of brethren. But if you aren't worthy, you will be food. May only the moon goddess have mercy on your soul because none can aide you in this challenge. Do you accept?" The Great Pirate King said many octaves lower.

"Yes my King. I wish to be fully part of your crew and the freedom it partakes in." Shortblade said with his voice shaking as his mighty chest inhaled and exhaled heavily.

The ruler of the seven seas our great and majestic Pirate King took Shortblade's hand and sliced it with the ceremonial silver dagger that burned in the King's hand as he griped it tightly. Then he threw the dagger into the huge bonfire instantly making an emerald smoke of magic appearing like some whimsical mist over the gasping crowd. The dagger then flew out of the fire across to a painted circle on a massive tree. The tree had risen above our courtyard facing the moon with a sundial's face and the dagger in the center; the shadow reflected the passing of time.

"Choose now a weapon from days of old my warrior and may your aim stay true. The game is on. Be the hunter or be hunted; tis' your birthright either way." The King darkly said as we all watched Shortblade scramble to choose a three spiked spear fashioned from King Neptune himself it was believed.

The Pirate King suddenly disappeared leaving an emerald puff of smoke as we watched Shortblade run into the jungle. Then we heard the werewolf's long terrifying howl and knew the chase had begun.

"Quick Lad let's go to the moors of the beach and we can watch above the cliffs at the outcome." Hatley whispered to me as he pulled my arm to follow him bringing a bottle of rum for each of us.

"But Hatley isn't that against the rules?" I whispered.

"Whoever told you that blarney? I watched you face the same tribulation." Hatley said in a hushed tone but chuckled.

My stomach became queasy as I remembered being cornered against the cliff walls as the beasts snout stopped on my chest breathing me in and baring its gigantic gnarly fangs. Its breath smelt of blood and brandy as the memory came flooding back I drank more and shuddered of that night.

"Wait Hatley, how do you know the wolf and Shortblade will end up there by the end of the night?" I asked as he led me high up on the cliffs in a treacherous climb above the sandy beach that the ocean rolls into softly.

We lay on our stomachs in the sweet grass, high on a cliff edge and far below us I could see the waves rolling over white sand. We faced another cliff edge that held a large curve in a semi-circle of a wall and at the bottom of the curve laid a huge pile of bones on the beach.

"Because the werewolf encircles each person the same way a predator directs food back to its lair to eat. Tis' the ultimate kill spot and the beast be' clever and been doing this for decades. Against that curved wall of the cliffs is where it decides your fate." Hatley whispered as he pulled out some biscuits for us to eat.

"We might be here for a bit, unless Shortblade isn't that great at escaping the beast. Might as well get cozy, it'll be a wait. Either way, when we hear the crunching of bones we will be able to see the outcome." Hatley said as he drank some rum, finished off a biscuit, and pulled the hat over his eyes.

It always amazed me how fast Hatley could fall asleep soundly and in a precarious situation none the less. The little butterfly fluttered its wings as he snored and I gasped as it transformed to a little fairy lady falling asleep in his long beard. I suddenly drank more rum as I watched the wee person with red hair and red dress, sweetly holding the beard in sleep too. Its tiny iridescent wings slightly shimmered in the moonlight as I watch both peaceful while sleeping on the edge of the cliff beside me.

It seemed like hours went by of screaming, howling, and growling noises on the island that seemed to be horrifically amplified. At one time I had even heard Shortblade loudly shriek as somewhere the beast must have caught him by surprise. But I eventually drifted off too, as the hours passed.

🌾🌾🌾

I awoke to the loud crunching of bones and someone jabbing me with their elbow hard.

"Ouch Hatley, that be a bruise in the morn." I said and giggled as I rubbed my ribcage.

"Hush now, there he be' frightened and cornered against the wall. Now watch the red-eyed werewolf move in to smell its prey's soul." Hatley said in a hushed tone.

"That's what it does? I always wondered why it breathed me in that night." I whispered back as we watched Shortblade running back and forth on the bones looking frantic.

"It's breathing in the light and darkness of your soul. And then it sees your soul's future." Hatley whispered.

"It sees your soul's future?" I asked as Shortblade spotted us in despair.

"Yes. But it also sees more. To past this test tis' not the vengeful heart or the blatant cruelness to harm a magical creature that lets you pass. Tis' always been the fragile heart that stands at the mouth of the beast. Even facing rows of fangs they show a kind of courage in knowing their end is near. They surrender to their ultimate death in a pure act of honor. They stand there against all odds; not running, not fighting, and not fearful. They are at peace with what is and the infinite unescapable death that comes for us all at the end of our lives." Hatley said as he looked down to Shortblade still running back and forth on the bones.

"I sees' it a million times and we both have lived through it. Arrrgghh." Hatley said and stiffened his back as we saw it.

The colossal werewolf looked frightening and ancient as it stood over nine feet tall with six-inch jagged-claws towering closer and closer to Shortblade. Suddenly the oversized demon-wolf dropped to all fours and moved slowly; closer and closer to Shortblade up with his back against the cliff wall.

His spear had been held high as we watched on but I covered my eyes and I was sure that Shortblade's eyes had been on me a moment before. I peeked through my fingers as Shortblade stood grasping the wall behind him for support.

"You have taken everything from me. He was the only thing I ever cared about and you murdered him. He was more beautiful than a warm sunrise and you ripped his heart out. I hate you. The only thing I have dreamt of these last days is ways to kill you. This weapon is pure silver and can do the job justly." Shortblade yelled at the approaching black furred monster from Hell with its red eyes glowing and its massive tail swishing.

A long murderous howl erupted from the fearsome creature making me and Hatley jump.

"But even killing you can't bring back my true love or even make him want to live for me. So…I offer you my life. It's the only thing I can think of that will stop my never ceasing pain." Shortblade shouted in anguish and then lowered his head as his arms stayed open in dropping the spear.

The creature of legend and the magical beast of myth rushed Shortblade just then going straight for his open heaving chest. All the while Shortblade's eyes remained closed and I held my breath.

CHAPTER 19

I heard the low grizzly growl and then a longer terrifying howl as I opened my eyes with a chill down my spine. In utter shock I watched the werewolf twisting and transforming in front of Shortblade's now wide eyes. Then there stood the Great Pirate King and my heart beat wildly as I watched him standing tall.

The Pirate King's proud character softened as he took Shortblade in his arms. And Shortblade wept while being held in the King's embrace.

"Let's go Lad as the dawn approaches. We need to join the circle to welcome him into the pack and our beloved clan." Hatley said and I looked at him and nodded while the orange butterfly in his beard fluttered its wings.

As we made our way through the forest Hatley left pants and a shirt at the start of the path to the castle. When I noticed the very fine silk shirt I smiled over to Hatley who winked as he pulled out a grand hat with light orange peacock feathers in it. His bag seemed to be magic as I would never have guessed all that, plus two bottles of rum and biscuits could fit in such a small satchel. We all looked out for each other. My family was the best; there was no doubt in my mind.

Once Hatley and I crossed the threshold of the courtyard there were men still chanting softly as the drums still beat that had been playing all night. Hatley raised his arms and without saying a word the music and drums beating; started playing louder.

Even though the daylight was upon us, it hadn't cracked through the gray clouds and Sully lit up the torches in the circle. More logs were added to the bonfire and the flames seemed to grow higher in the sight of the Pirate King escorting our new brethren into the circle. The substantial ancient tree holding the moon-dial with dagger showed the dawns rays as it descended down to normalness and it magically chimed that time was up.

A loud hush came over us as the Pirate King raised his arm and the dagger floated to his hand. Shortblade immediately kneeled bowing his head low and the Pirate King stood smiling as his fangs elongated. Then lightning cracked the sky as his captivating eyes glowed red. The Pirate King raised his grand dagger high above his head as lightning struck the blade turning the silver into a burning blue flame.

"Shortblade has proven himself worthy and is indeed part of our faithful crew and family for life. He is under our protection. Show him the way men and show him some congratulations for now he is ours." The Pirate King said as he kissed the jewel encrusted blade of his dagger and then placed it on the kneeling bowed head of Shortblade as we cheered.

The Great Pirate King spoke in some ancient language as he sliced his right hand and then took Shortblade's right hand slicing it in the same fashion. The Pirate King chanted a mantra as he placed his hand to

Shortblade's hand and the blood dripped down. While the pirate brethren, including myself, sliced our own hands and lined up to bond our blood with his hand saying the blood oath to our kindred spirit;

"Pirate blood brothers till the grave and beyond;

We sail together and we live for sacred treasure;

Death before dishonor ever;

For the rogue winds and fair sails;

For the strong rum and tall tales;

We pledge our souls to our brethren bond."

As I approached Shortblade's smiling face I held his hand to mine and said the blood pledge to him with all of my heart. He made the same blood vow to me. But I also whispered in his ear; "I knew you could do it my friend." His eyes glistened in happiness.

After we all had said the blood bond in shaking Shortblade's hand we re-pledged our blood bond to the Pirate King in shaking his hand. As I pledged my blood bond to the Pirate King his red eyes glowed brighter and I brought his hand to my heart. Time stood still as his dreamy eyes said I love you to mine and my heart raced for his. I stepped back into the waiting circle of crewmen but couldn't stop looking at how magmatic my King truly was.

Then the Pirate King waved his hand high speaking an ancient language and spell cast. Our hands glowed and a spooky green mist hovered as everyone's wounds healed.

Then a loud holler and cheer came from Hatley and everyone cheered. Now the celebration would come of Shortblade finally joining us. My heart seemed to burst as he was welcomed with open arms to our family.

But I noticed around the courtyard where five sad men sat, who hadn't taken the bravery test and were not able to join in the blood oath.

But you had to take the true test of your soul or else you weren't fully immersed into the crew's warmth. It was the only way to measure a man's heart and the loyalty inside. And without that act of courage you were just another sailor.

I raised my mug to Shortblade with everyone and he ecstatically smiled back drinking heartily. Meanwhile I noticed what seemed like a flash of distaste in O'Shady's eyes and then it was gone. He was part of the men who hadn't taken the blood oath and I wished that tonight he would have joined the family. The Pirate King never forced anyone to join us but standing among my fellow brethren it was clear that this was an honor. I couldn't understand how anyone wouldn't want to be a part of our great pirate clan.

The morning of dark magic swirled and intensified as we sang our favorite sea shanties and drank merrily in this occasion of victory and triumph gaining another member of our family and pirate shipmate for life.

⸙⸙⸙⸙

CHAPTER 20

I awoke in the meadow as the sun was setting; surrounded by daisies, orchids, wild roses, and heavy snoring. I wasn't sure how I had wondered off but I lay happy in the strong arms that held me snug and sat up stretching. It was quite a peculiar sight as I awoke with Dragon hanging his heavy arm around me and I could see my breath in the air. But I could feel someone's breath by my feet holding my legs.

I'm not sure what had happened last night but there was a bunch of us in the field in a row, all fully clothed and snoring soundly. Shortblade lay by my feet. His blonde hair was golden in the twilight of the sun setting. *What a party. We must have slept all day. Tis' exactly how my initiation ended when I became a pirate and fully embraced by the brethren. I wonder if the magic and celebration takes us away in the moment or if someone spiked the rum again with fairy magic?*

Fairy magic was a potent thing as it wasn't meant for humans or immortals. The effects sometimes lasted for days of headaches and vomiting pink juices periodically. I sighed as I watched Shortblade turn and puke a pinkish fluid.

I looked over and seen the fairy laughing in Hatley's beard. She was in a hysterical roll of laughter and not paying attention. I snuck up and captured her in my hands which completely wiped the smile off her face.

"This is treachery and you know it. I shall slit your throat so you will stop torturing us." I said to her while shaking my head and grabbing my dagger out of my belt.

The sweet face started crying and shaking her head in pleading. I really liked the fae of the island even in there mischievous ways but we were supposed to ship out. And now everyone would be seasick before we even boarded Telulahs Revenge. *This wasn't the best time for fairy tricks.* I thought as I raised my dagger for the good of all the men. The little fairy was so beautiful in a red silk dress and iridescent wings; making my hand wet with her light purple tears. But it was always duty before hearts desires and the men needed a break from her witchcraft.

I closed my eyes raising my dagger high but my blade stopped as someone's hand touched mine.

"You mustn't. Though she is a devil and a pixie; I have befriended her. If you kill her; it be' the knife you plunge into my chest not hers." Hatley said gently and I dropped the dagger to the grass.

"Oh Hatley, she poisoned us again though." I said frustrated but relieved. It was way too early in the late afternoon to be killing rogue fairies.

"Arrrgghh, I know. But it has also made us tolerant and immune to dying from the fairy drink. She has been doing it to us for years making our bodies fight that death. Be kind to her, though she be a trickster she shows us mercy." Hatley said sternly.

"Mercy?" I said understanding Hatley but not really.

"Yes, because if she wanted us dead she would have done it long ago." Hatley said and I passed him the little fairy that kissed his cheek and transformed into a butterfly.

"I guess you were right Hatley. She was stealing rum from you all this time." I said with a laugh.

Hatley laughed too and passed me the bottle. I looked at him in an unsure glance clutching my stomach as I ran to the opposite side of everyone and puked pink fluid up. *Jeeze, it sucked being poisoned. But Hatley was right. I felt pretty good now that I vomited. My stomach must be amazing in tolerating fairy poison by now.* I just finished thinking that thought when I vomited even more pink glittery fluid.

"Easy Lad." Hatley said as he helped me up and then went over to rub Shortblade's back.

"I'm okay." I said and wiped my mouth on my sleeve creating a pink shimmered streak on my forearm.

It was kind of pretty to look at as it glittered in the setting sun. Too bad I knew the truth of the situation and the dazzling pink all over Shortblade's shirt. He looked really rough this late afternoon. But he was with us and he'd be alright. Because if I could develop the tolerance quickly I knew he could. *That damn pixie's been poisoning us for years.* I thought and laughed.

It was going to be a great night.

⁂

CHAPTER 21

Through the evening we packed Telulahs Revenge with light supplies. And we set off to sail into the darkness where the sea monster was waiting in the deception of the deep just off the wharf. We sent a small unmanned row boat off in her direction while we sailed the other way. We had to leave a rag from the Pirate Kings clothes as a decoy. Our tricks always worked surprisingly over the years, but something had changed in the terrifying creature of the sea.

We were now able to easily put great distance between us. I looked over the edge of the boat and noticed a giant dark green sea tentacle severed and floating on the ocean's ceiling. It made me shudder as I took the nest. She hadn't been in a battle since our last escape and even then it wasn't our cannons that had hurt Telulah, it was the Royal Guard gunning for her when they were chasing us. She had caught them. But the battle had taken its toll on her. She was definitely moving much slower this last year and I wondered if it was the magic dying inside her or her mortal heart. *Can Telulahs hate keep her going through many more years of battles and many years of loneliness? Love is what keeps me going, I know thyself. But what of hate? I think hate breaks thee down like a fine poison rotting you from thy inside out. I think Telulahs hate is finally killing her. She's not healing anymore.* I pondered to myself as I looked to the sea and then back to the small boat.

I looked out at the horizon as we made headway. Our sturdy vessel I never questioned because we all had bled and sweat over her keep, with honor and pride. *Telulahs Revenge is more than our pirate ship. Our ship holds the beating heart of every crew on board.* I thought as I looked down at our war bringer with my heart in bloom. She was our refuge holding our ghost stories; our secrets; and all our dreams of unfathomable treasure. It wasn't hard to love something so amazing even though it be' inanimate. The weathered wood had changed over the years but our ship's heart strummed through the night and our black sails flew high.

A million stars lit up the sky and I felt like I was overlooking my heaven as I scanned the horizon. Clear skies and smooth sailing; and a perfect moment at sea. The sea air was always brisk and I smelt deeply the salty wind that took my breath and filled my lungs as big as the sails. *What a glorious night to be at sea.* I thought as I kept an eye on the beast now far away from us and happy in destroying our decoy boat.

"That a girl Telulah. Okay men, listen up. We sail to London for supplies and then we sail to treasure. Bear away onto a broad reach on starboard tack. Dismissed." The Captain's deep voice rang true through the night.

"Yay." All the crew cheered and hollered as the Captain had said the magic word to ignite us all into working harder on the ship.

I looked down smiling at the wide grins on everyone's faces in the pure happiness and excitement of gold or jewels. We never questioned what the treasure was. It really didn't matter. Because everyone got a cut and this was what we lived for. And I couldn't wait.

I noticed Shortblade working closely with crewmate Sully and they were teasing each other. Crewmate Sully had started around the same time as me but he was closer to Shortblade and the Captain's age. He had been a sailor with another terrible crew of pirates before they all were captured. He was daring and full of brawn. I liked him a lot because he seemed to have the spirit of a joyous elf. He was always cracking jokes but worked very hard too. As I watched them what really made me smile was crewmate Sully had placed his hand on Shortblade's hip to help sturdy him with the ease of the sheets. But his hand stayed there lingering after they were finished. I saw them wink at each other while no one noticed and then I started to scan the horizon again with a smile.

We sailed by the wind and the stars. There wasn't ever a time frame because we would just stop at port and pillage if we ran out of supplies. *Truly tis' a glorious life.* I looked down at Hatley at the helm while our glorious Captain was going below. I saw him look at me and wink as I tipped my hat in respect with a smile.

🌱🌱🌱🌱

There were two crews one was day and one was night. Hatley was the first mate and in charge of the night crew. It was fair winds all night but I winced at the red sun that arose as I descended the main mast and crewmate O'Shady greeted me in taking the nest. The shift change was smooth but I was beat and weary with that cursed red sun; and dark clouds over portside. I had faith in our men and in our ship but sleeping through a hurricane was never easy.

I went to my little bunk off the Captain's private quarters and drifted to sleep. I felt his lips on my cheek for a moment and an extra blanket gently moved over my shivering body.

⁂

A month went by of cabin duties, blood gifts, and secret rendezvous with my love. It was always just after shift change; our hidden intimacy stole away moments of a cherished space between our hearts and endearing kisses. And it made time on the ship even grander.

We had sailed to London many times but sometimes we would get stuck in the doldrums. In those times we would practice sword techniques while we waited for the winds to catch sail. And that was the only reason our voyage ever took longer; that and the sea monster that plagued our existence every time we entered the open water. We often changed course or docked at different tropical islands to lose the creature briefly. But it was like her navigation was tuned into us. Actually I think it was the Captain. *I wonder if a broken heart ever truly beats again?* I thought as I watched Shortblade practicing a duel with Sully. They were having great fun laughing and besting each other. It seemed that their laughter was too jolly and O'Shady came up from below with an awful scowl as his blonde hair was a mess and dark circles under his eyes creased as large as the frown on his face.

I ignored his displeasure and laughed at their good sportsmanship in the cool early morning air. Then I looked over at far horizon and saw Telulahs great tangle of horns splash out of the water and I frowned as I watched her one great clawed fin clutching another monster of the deep. All the men stopped to watch the sea beast eating a giant shark almost the size of her massive dragon head. I suddenly became chilled as even though she was more than 15,000 fathoms away; her eerie glowing eyes were on us. Those massive yellow lanterns never slept and always pointed in our direction. *I wondered how long ago this chase had begun and if Telulah would catch us one day even if she only had one clawed hand-like fin?* I pondered this as the sun was slowly creeping up and I saw land on the horizon.

"Land hoy." I shouted as the men cheered and the Captain appeared on the deck looking quite dashing.

I shivered as I climbed down the mast and passed O'Shady in our usually morning musings. He seemed grumpier than normal but with land in sight it had boosted his spirit. But looking at the monster stirred the memory of our last encounter. We were being tortured in the brigs when Telulah crashed into us. The Royal Guard had been ready as Telulah came for us but who can ever be that ready when it comes to a giant sea dragon?

While they fought her off we barely escaped through the open holes in the boat. She destroyed the Royal Guard's three ships like they were toys. When she had feasted on men and wood; the smell was devastating and imprinted on my brain. It smelt worse than the thousands of lost souls hanging off the weeping willow in the mermaid's lagoon. I shivered again as I felt a hand pat my back.

"Dragonfly, the beast may catch us one day. But never fear our destiny. It is what shapes our course and path in life. Fear stops you from living and there are millennia of lives yet to live." The Captain spoke softly to me as he stood beside me on the deck.

Without any words we watched the beast even further and further away as our fast ship sailed. I looked over to his pale blue eyes that seemed grim as we came into the soup around the waters of London. I made my way below as the Captain took the helm steering the ship towards the secret passages. It wouldn't be long before we would be in the safe haven of Cut-Throat Kathleen's brothel and bath house; in the quiet countryside of Trenton. And I couldn't wait.

I went to the galley to eat with the rest of the men and Hatley asked me to bring Shortblade his breakfast as he had went to a separate part of the bottom of the ship where supplies were kept but also a makeshift room for ill crew. As I carried the tray down, past the crew's quarters and way down in the belly of the ship I could hear muffled sounds.

I stopped as I heard the passionate sounds of quiet moans. The door lay ajar as I watched glistening muscular skin strewn with beaded sweat and ravishing hands. The lovers frantically kissed each other grabbing tightly the yearnings they hoped would keep them atoned for another day. I held my breath in this knowledge of intimacy because it was exactly what the Captain and I had been doing. *I think that sometimes the heart grows a need that you can't fight off. What are we in this world without love?* I thought of these things as I heard them whispering in the sweetness of love murmurs and didn't want to disturb them. I placed the tray of food on the stairs and purposefully knocked a large caldron over so they could have their dignity. I pretended to just come down the stairs picking up the tray before Sully came out with his skin still glistening. His pants hung heavy slightly below his hips and he couldn't hide the panting as he stood before my blush. He had always been a pure powerhouse of athleticism; but breathed so hearty you swear he had run a lap around the boat.

"Oh you brought the food for Shortblade that is wonderful. I was just going to get him something to eat as he is pretty weak still." Sully said almost out of breath as I passed him the tray.

"Can you take it to him? I will let Hatley know you are helping him and he needs more rest. That way no one will disturb him." I said and held an expression of worry.

"Yes, I will help spoon-feed him. I think tis' best if he wasn't disturbed. He is in a weakened state. After all, no one wants to catch the flu do they?" Sully said with a half-hearted laugh.

"Certainly not. I will make sure the crew doesn't come down here. There is some rainwater if he needs a quick refresh. Bring up the dishes when you can. Thank you for helping our fellow mate Sully." I sincerely said and passed him the tray.

"It is my pleasure in helping him well. Our bond is forever." Sully said and placed his right hand over his heart while balancing the tray.

I nodded with my right hand over my heart and turned to go up the stairs. But I turned back to watch Sully carrying the tray slowly to the room and my heart almost burst as he stopped to kiss the apple before placing it back on the tray of food. His smile was so warm and it amazed me how much he actually cared. But he reserved this side of his brawn; the world rarely saw this strength on his outside fierce appearance. It was too bad the world was cruel to the best of us. To look at Sully was to gaze upon a cold handsomeness. His fierce expression frightened many but when he spoke he was poetic and gentle. He had a long scar down his right eye and I was thankful, the cruel world hadn't changed his covered heart. *We are the judged and the vicious pirates of the seas. Why is it we all hide? We are already outcasts. I just want to live and be happy and be free. Is it so wrong to long for such happiness or tis' out of reach just like the closest guiding star?* I thought as I went back through the cabin and then into the galley speaking to Hatley about Shortblade still being ill. Hatley gave the order not to disturb Shortblade so he can rest and we all wouldn't risk falling to illness. Now Sully would be given the caring duties of bringing food and necessities to Shortblade; until he was better or land hoy. And I felt pure joy enter my heart at Shortblade not being alone but did not express the sentiment on my cold face.

🌾🌾🌾🌾

We left our ship in the harbor and made our way on the small boats carrying what little belongings we needed. But our long dark coats and boots were undeniable as our fierce faces looked into the quietness of the land. The plan was a short overnight stay to steal the map, to the great treasure.

We all had stowed away weapons hidden under our garments. In particular, I always kept a dagger in each boot and one in my belt along with two sets of key-picks. My key-picks were the other love of my life and I was able to get in and out of any locked apparatus. I had one set of key-picks in my boot and another set hidden in my garter belt along with a very small vile of poison Hatley had given me. Even though I was wearing baggy pants; one pocket had a hole that fit my hand through in a bind. My bow and arrows I had brought as a just in case but left them in my leather satchel under the overturned boat.

Everyone wore their sword under their coat sheathed in their belts in case we had to draw fast. Not everyone in are party had a musket, only a few. It was because the damn guns took forever to load in hand to hand combat. They were great with cannons on the ship and attacking another ship but were useless in hand to hand combat.

The road from the boats was riddled with wet beach sand and crab grass. I hadn't seen many horse carriages come this way in the past and even the path lay vacant now. *This path is just as vast and empty as the ocean. And just the way I like.* I thought as I side glanced the empty tree line but watched a deer jump out and then heard someone's gun go off.

"Damn, bullet's lost to the bark." O'Shady said sheepishly.

"Try not to waste bullets on the trees men." Hatley said and rolled his eyes.

But I looked over at Hatley and we both smiled at the same time. This wasn't the first time or the last time someone fired their musket prematurely and I held back my snickers.

"And don't bring attention to ourselves men. We only have one night here and bounties on all our heads. And instead of the dungeons I wish to spend it in many sweet ladies arms' if you please." Hatley said in his stern voice that was scolding us before we even got into trouble.

The plan was simple enough. Half the crew was going with the Pirate King to acquire the hidden map at the Duke of Trenton's Castle and the other half was going to Cut-Throat Kathleen's brothel to lay invisibly low.

The Duke of Trenton's Castle was not even worth my great talent of lock picking. He was inviting of the pirates and always too drunk to ever notice what went missing. He kept his treasure maps on the floor strewn about his library not believing their worth; they were never locked up. And I smiled at the break I was catching because the brothel was a whole lot more fun.

It was known that singing and dancing awaited Cut-Throat Kathleen's fine establishment with more women than any of the men knew what to do with. By Neptune, I didn't even know what you'd do with three women at one time but Hatley sure did. It was always a real good time even with a clear average of three bar fights a night. But it was by far still the better choice, than the boring Dukes.

I watched the Pirate King leave with my heart and with the day crew down a different path. I tipped my hat to them as they left. The Pirate King smiled and gave me a nod as they ducked back into the shadows of a covered up path leading into some thick trees.

We continued way down the road with huge grins.

"The Captain told me specifically that we cannot bring attention to ourselves. Arrrgghh, but he also said we could let our sea-legs out." Hatley said and winked.

"Yay." We all cheered as we stepped lighter in being off duty.

I missed my King but couldn't hustle any faster to the brothel. *God*

I love being a pirate. I thought and as soon as we gave the secret knock; the door opened with booming cheers galore. Hatley was flooded with women aplenty. They flocked to his long red beard like magic.

All the men were bombarded with frilly high skirts, big mugs and beautiful curves; including myself. I quickly let the ladies poetically down by telling them I was only drinking tonight with a wink.

There were other pirates docked for the night and it was great seeing the hard faces I hadn't seen in years.

While we all heavily drank a fun local named; *'Tiger-fanged Tommy'* was on the piano playing up a storm. Cut-Throat Kathleen made her famous stew for us without the rabbit fur this time and we ate with even more cheers all around. We were getting fabulously drunk and the night had only begun. *I love being a pirate.* I thought as I twirled off the chandelier upside down and everyone cheered.

❋❋❋

CHAPTER 22

Cut-Throat Kathleen's brothel was the place to be in this small shire of countryside away from the hustle and bustle of the budding towns and villages. The Duke of Trenton owned the surrounding lands and castles; and was not a pillar of society. He had the royal title but no intentions of ruling the lands. He had to take orders from the Evil King Vermin of Bristol and loathed those rare occasions. But for the most part this was considered outlaw territory and untouchable. There were far too many of us pirates to capture but the evil King Vermin had been trying for years sending his merciless Royal Guard after us.

This brothel was known only to pirates and had a secret entrance that couldn't be found by the average street urchin. It was our personal hangout. It seemed the Pirate King had funded this establishment and saved the ruthless women who ran the house. There was a rumor that her family had been somehow related to the Pirate King but no one dared to ask questions. She was hard from years of peace keeping between the concubines and other men that visited the joint. But I knew she loved me from the very first days of being brought in when the Pirate King had saved me from the gutter of the alley of death. He had stopped here for the night before boarding the ship and Cut-Throat Kathleen having never had any children of her own helped me like I was part of her kin. From the very first broth she served me; I knew she cared deeply for me. I think she even knew of my hidden condition and was still a loyal heart. But to everyone else you couldn't cross her. Her vengefulness was unrelenting and as merciless as the sea monster.

Even more ladies flocked to Hatley as I heard his jolly bellied laughter from across the bar. I do believe they were getting him drunk as a few ladies were pulling his coat gently up the stairs to a waiting room. The little butterfly stayed fluttering its wings in his beard and I smiled at him drinking rum while trying to go up the stairs. He was looking at me with such a deliriously happy expression and winked at me as he was willingly dragged inside a room.

I had the biggest grin on my face and looked over to Shortblade who had his arms crossed while he sat on the stool at the bar. He didn't seem to be having any fun as he continued to get wasted. I saw him watch Sully go laughing into a room with a maiden and he frowned even more deeply.

His perfect face had a healed cut under his eye that I think made him even more dashing as he finished two glasses and then got another. I sat beside him and clanged my mug to his and he gave me a sad cheers.

I looked over the crowd and at Madeira ignoring everyone; she was walking slowly with intent and seduced all the men she passed. She was far too beautiful to be in this establishment and knew it. You had to give everything and your soul to be with her. And even then her superficial heart only liked handsomeness. While her fine dress swayed back and forth over to Shortblade's bar stool he was still looking at me with this bored but lonely expression.

"Ahoy there aren't you a sight to gaze upon. Come with me now and let us talk about a sophistication that these simpletons will never know. I can see by the lace ribbon in your blonde locks that you are noble in birth." Madeira said to Shortblade with an accent as sweet as honey that made the other men drool.

Her rosy lips were plump and wet as she looked like she was almost cooing over him. She intentionally dabbed her handkerchief to her breasts and neck. Then she dropped the handkerchief.

"Oh, I declare." Madeira softly gasped and Shortblade picked it up while she pretended to adjust her stockings in front of him and lifted her skirt high as he passed it back with a smile.

"Here you are my fairest of ladies." Shortblade said and bowed genuine to her.

Then he looked over to me very unimpressed at my grin and this trap he was in. I watched her move closer firmly planting her robust cleavage against his arm that held his drink. She was stealth like in capturing her prey and yet soft enough not to spill his drink. I had seen this many times before and smiled even larger at what was happening. Her actions always worked, no man could resist Madeira. He was her new toy as the crew's newest official shipmate and he was fresh meat. She kissed him placing his hand to her cleavage in sealing the deal and then led him away to a private room up the stairs.

He looked back to me with a half-smile and I held my mug up to him in a toast.

"Come on Lad sing us a song. We need some lively entertainment." Cut-Throat Kathleen said husky as her words slurred a little and she grabbed me in a hug placing me up on the bar.

"Yes, don't make us beg to hear your voice of an angel Dragonfly."

Tiger-fanged Tommy said as he started playing the upbeat intro, dressing the piano keys up in pizazz as his fingers flew across the ivory.

"Yes Dragonfly, sing us a happy song." Someone in the crowd said lively.

And all the men cheered as I bowed to them and finished my mug of rum.

"Yes my men, for the love of you and for the love of the sea." I shouted and then started dancing a jig to the music.

"For the love of you and the love of the sea." Everyone repeated as they toasted me and started clapping or stomping their feet to the beat.

One of the most beautiful ladies joined me up on the bar in dancing as I started singing the sea shanty I wrote. Everyone was hooting and moving their mugs in merriment as I started to sing;

"Oh ta-do-la-do-la day,

Oh ta-do-la-do-la day. (The crowd sang with me)

The fearsome Captains' going a courting;

Oh ta-do-la-do-la day,

Hatley's dark rum has been a thwarting.

Oh ta-do-la-do-la day,

Oh ta-do-la-do-la day. (The crowd sang with me)

A merry pirate's life of treasure;

Oh ta-do-la-do-la day,

The scanty sea be' our only pleasure.

Oh ta-do-la-do-la day,

Oh ta-do-la-do-la day. (The crowd sang with me)

The frivolous winds a beauty be';

Oh ta-do-la-do-la day,

The Royal Guard's pay a higher fee.

Oh ta-do-la-do-la day,

Oh ta-do-la-do-la day. (The crowd sang with me)

When we catch them we'll slit their throats;

Oh ta-do-la-do-la day,

Telulah eats and eats their boats. (Men cheered.)

Oh ta-do-la-do-la day,

Oh ta-do-la-do-la day. (The crowd sang with me)

The Pirate Kings blood lust takes its toll;

But his black soul is ours and makes our hearts full.

(All the men cheered a big hooray.)

Oh ta-do-la-do-la day, (Everyone sang)

Oh ta-do-la-do-la day, (Everyone sang)

Oh ta-do-la-do-la day, (Everyone sang)

Oh ta-do-la-do-la day. (Everyone sang and mugs clanked)"

I did a couple of cartwheels and a flip as everyone cheered me on while the chorus and music carried on. I looked up as the piano tempo kept going and I could hear others singing the chorus still. Then I jumped to the chandelier and hung upside down as it spun.

Shortblade I just noticed was standing in the door frame looking at me with his mouth open in shock as I smiled up to him. His bare chest glistened with sweat dripping down his muscular body and his pants barely hung off his beautiful hips. His long blonde hair was loose and heavenly. I could see Madeira in the bed sleeping as he continued to stare at me, now back on the bar dancing to the new music that continued to play, while the men cheered and swung their mugs.

Shortblade had this look of fear in his eyes but I ignored it as Kathleen came to me and tapped my shoe.

"Now do the other one I love." Cut-Throat Kathleen shouted over the piano.

The tempo changed slow and hauntingly beautiful as Tiger-fanged Tommy gave into his mistress's wishes.

"Yes do that one Dragonfly. It seems a love story full of magic." A lovely lady named Melody shouted from the balcony grabbing Shortblade's arm just because he was there. Her negligée revealed everything including her bare soul as she clung to him and he placed his arm around her frailness in comfort.

But all the eyes were on me as the tempo moved slower and I sang of my heartbreak;

"The stars would fall before I seen your smile again there;
My loving heart calls to you but you don't care.
My heart is deep and true because I dare;
But you are lost to me forever and the kindness we share.

'Cause when I kissed you, you went away,
The blood lust and the sea is where you'll stay.
Where did you go? Where did my love go?

Far from me into the deepest of the blue,
My bared soul and eternal love; you hadn't a clue.
I gave my all and off the plank my heart you threw,
Into the deepest grave my death it grew.

'Cause when I kissed you, you went away,
The blood lust and the sea is where you'll stay.
Where did you go? Where did my love go?

Our souls were tied in secret we in heat lay,
To the barnacles of hell, alone we will stay.

Wounded by your refusal is a slow death of your plague,
My dying heart is withered and sails scorched in a fray.

'Cause when I kissed you, you went away,
The blood lust and the sea is where you'll stay.
Where did you go? Where did my love go?

I surrender to the sweet mercy of my grim endless test;
To join your doom my love, I'll be the golden treasure of your best.
With this unpolished silver dagger I plunge forever in my chest;
I'll slay our love in killing my heart's pain and unrest.

Because an eternity without you I cannot hope to even bare;
And our vast blue love is that out of reach sapphire rare.
All the stars fall around me as I dream of your ended heart fair.

'Cause when I kissed you, you went away,
The blood lust and the sea is where you'll stay.
Where did you go? Where did my love go?"

As I finished I looked out into the crowd of tears. The whole mood had changed to sorrow as the ladies were crying and the men grunted and wiped trickles of tears. Some men hurriedly declined with a sobbing escort to one of the many waiting rooms. I watched as Shortblade had been wiping his tears away and Melody's as her face was now on his chest. His frown grew as he held her and she clung to him.

I felt the same way as tears now were down my face.

We all knew our chosen outcome. Our lives did not consist of the normal societal happy endings. No marriage with children and no true love were in our future. We were all married to the merciless sea and the life of piracy was that damned care free. The wind and the waves called to our souls as much as we all liked to dream of a never-ending passionate love. Treasure and friendship was all the currency in our blood, any of us could ever hold. And it was guarded by our beating dragons in our caged chests. We would live and die for each other just to keep the only thing touchable in relation to family we could ever hope for.

I smiled sadly as I scanned the crowd and then gasped as I saw the menacing looking Pirate King. The sadness of the sun crew stood beside us. He was fuming with his boot tapping on the floor and a hush went over the crowd as his icy blue eyes looked at me flashing a red warning. His fangs were extended over his long frowned lips and still held the blood of someone.

Gasping, I jumped down from the bar. They must have been standing there in the entrance because the sun crew's faces frowned and their eyes glistened.

A sped up tempo played on the piano to liven things a bit while I could hear the dark voice of the Pirate King scolding Cut-Throat Kathleen and Hatley as he had come down from the commotion.

"For Hades sake, I could hear Dragonfly singing about slicing the Royal Guard's throats just like all of bloody London." The Pirate King roared with a deepening growl in his throat that seemed unearthly.

It was easy to see that I was in trouble next, so I slipped out the backdoor with the bottle of rum Kathleen had given me earlier. I ran from the bar to the overturned boat on the beach and slid on my belly to hide underneath. I knew the Pirate King could easily find me but I hoped it would buy me some time so he could cool off. And I needed alone time. I was still sad about the song I had written from my own despair and wanted to drown my sorrow.

I had written the song about the love I had in my heart for the Pirate King that could never be unless I gave up my secret. I continued to drink as I lay on my stomach watching the water and slow waves creep up to the shore. I wondered what it would have been like to have his children. I wondered if they would have his good looks and fiery temper. I dreamt of how beautiful our children would have been.

"My love hiding from me won't distract my temper…I…I smell blood. An inescapable amount of carnage is happening right now. We shall have this discussion later. Stay hidden my Pet and I shall draw them away from thee. I will love you forever my Darling." The Pirate King's dark voice sounded even more mysterious than usual.

I mouthed the words '*I love you*' before feeling his lips to mine and then felt the absence of his heart as a chill ran down my spine.

🌿🌿🌿

CHAPTER 23

Coughing heavy I awoke to the harsh smell of ash and timber burning. The generous amount of black smoke was more than worrisome as I grabbed my satchel of quills and my bow. I slowly walked down the beach and then ran in the direction of the thick black smoke. I gasped and hid behind a tree as soon as I caught wind of the dresses swaying beside the nearby branches.

The lifeless bodies and soot-filled frilly skirts were swaying with their blue toes dangling amongst the leaves rustling in the unforgiving wind. Cut-Throat Kathleen's body was hanging from the tree but her head lay on the ground in a horrific expression. My tears streaked down my cheeks silently as I overheard the Royal Guards laughing.

"Like sitting geese, they was. This crew be' easier to slaughter than last time." One Royal Guard said as I watched him slide his hand on some blue toes and then disappear up the skirt.

"Roy don't be sick. These hags were with the pirates last night.

Good thing we were tipped off. It's a grand thing knowing how to kill the Great Sun-Dancer King." The other Royal Guard said as he punched the Guard named Roy hard in the arm.

"Yep, that blonde rogue was paid handsomely." Roy the Royal Guard ignored the punch and slowly removed his hand smelling his fingers than curled up his nose.

My whole face turned in disgust. *And they consider the Sun Dancer King a monster. He is more a man than they will ever hope to become.* Just then a tiny kitten came out of the bushes startled and the guards gushed over the small creature turning their backs from where I stood. My heart ached in hearing about the death of my love and something in me snapped.

My sadness instantly dissipated and I became suddenly furious. Blindly hating these guards; I pulled two arrows out of my canvas satchel and with one shot struck each through the back of their skulls. They didn't even have time to gasp as they died before they hit the ground and the kitten ran off. *Blonde rogue? Two crewmates I know who has blonde tassels.* I thought as I walked over to the tavern that was still burning. I felt my eyes red with the flames as I looked for anyone still breathing.

"Move and you're dead Dragonfly" The man's voice was hushed as it covered my mouth gently.

"Shortblade I'm going to kill you. How could you betray us?" I said as I bit down hard on his soft hand.

"Ouch that really hurts Dragonfly. I could not. I didn't do this. I took an oath with you and I choose to honor the code." Shortblade sounded hurt.

"Where are they? How did you escape?" I said panicked.

"Madeira convinced me to go to town to her place for more privacy because she caught me with sweet Melody. I only remember our love making and then blacked-out. She drugged me and I awoke alone;

robbed of all my possessions including my fine ribbon. She was long gone too, when I awoke. I came here to get answers and happened upon the same vile you have just seen." Shortblade said as his voice cracked.

I turned suddenly and seen the truth in his sad blue eyes. He hugged me and I hugged him back.

"Madeira is a snake and a dark-hearted mistress of the damned. If I see her again I shall slice her throat for your mishap." I said and stepped back from him as my anger still burned along with the building.

"We have to find out where the survivors are. They said they killed the Captain but the others will be somewhere. There's a blacksmith in town that makes us swords and the Evil King Vermin. We shall go there and find out from him where they are keeping our clan." I said as I gathered another broad sword and some daggers.

"How do you know they aren't all dead already?" Shortblade whispered.

"I don't see any of them hanging from the trees, do you? Besides, the Evil King Vermin indulgently hates us. We pirates are the bane on his perfect existence and killing us slowly is the only thing that will feed his sadistic soul. He will want to publicly display and advertise our torture." I said hotly as I looked down to Cut-Throat Kathleen's severed head.

I knelt down and kissed her cold face before I stormed back to the boat with Shortblade trying to keep up.

Just as we were getting any extra weapons and cloaks from the overturned boats we heard the cannons go off. My heart bottomed out as I watched Telulahs Revenge being blasted by the Royal Guards small fleet. But what happened next froze me and Shortblade grabbed my arm in being startled. On the horizon where our boat was being ravished with bombs; massive tentacles crashed against the warped boards. The giant squid-like arms wrapped around our vessel in the harbor easily dragging it to the locker. Then the immense sea creature destroyed the Royal Guards six ships that had turned their cannons to it.

"No." I shouted and dropped to my knees.

"Pull it together Dragonfly, that monster has been chasing us since before I joined the crew. It follows us from the tropics. We need to worry about saving the men." Shortblade said sharply and shook me hard.

"Listen, I'm sorry. But you were losing it." He said softer and helped me up.

"We need a plan and for you to stop acting like a girl because I need a skilled man by my side right now." Shortblade said and my eyes went wide.

"I have an idea that might work. But we have to work together." I said and looked at his puzzled expression.

He followed close as we moved through the morning fog silently to the blacksmith's abode. Our dark cloaks blended in the shadows as we silently made our way. But underneath the darkness of my cloak I held my bow with an arrow aching to draw the Royal Guards blood at first chance.

CHAPTER 24

Just like all the other village idiots; these two Royal Guards were a truly ignorant bunch and held no respect for anyone as they openly conversed in front of Shortblade and I. The courtyard was empty but you could see down the alleyway a huge crowd of peasants starting to gather in the center square where the wooden structure of the gallows was being built. Beside that was the Evil King Vermin's royal seat, upon a stage much higher than the courtyard. The Evil King Vermin had expanded his armies quickly and inadequately trained the middleclass peasants so they could feed his army of disposables. The Evil King would keep his knights close for show but there was no one else guarding the prison except these two pawns.

These two men guarding the prison were clearly a bunch of yeomen and a bunch of unskilled buffoons. But they were completely enamored with Shortblade. They recklessly discussed their future actions and I was grateful my crewmate was indeed so glamourous. We would use it to turn our fortune.

I made a curtsey so low my powdered cleavage almost popped out. Shortblade stood there with his leg bent as he fixed his stocking and garter belt boldly in front of the men. As Shortblade giggled he kissed me unexpectedly and in a heated passion while squeezing my large breasts hard. And as I kissed him back I caught his quick wink; but he continued to take my breath away with his steamy kisses. I felt feverish in this moment even though tis' a grand act. *Shortblade closes his eyes in each kiss and stolen touch. He kissed Philip exactly how he is kissing me right now. I remember seeing him with his passionate love.*

"This is total horse manure. Why should the prisoner's get visits by these lovely wenches?" The Guard spoke while he grabbed Shortblade's butt firm.

Shortblade giggled as he fluttered his fan. His powdered cleavage was very muscular and I was grateful he lacked an abundance of body hair for his manly age of twenty-three. With his paint he looked vivacious and his blonde hair was perfectly curled with a lace ribbon. We had both borrowed dresses and corsets that made Shortblade look ravishing to the Guards who in fact had a hard time keeping their hands now off him. And although I had to reassure Shortblade's ego that he looked stunning as a lady; Shortblade held more confidence in his lace, than I.

"The prisoners are all headed for the gallows at noon. The priest is letting them have one last earthly pleasure. Besides with twenty six pirates and the dead Sun Dancer King, I doubt these concubines will have lasting power. The carrion is starting to smell worse than the burnt bodies at the brothel we set aflame in the morn." The other Guard said as he stood holding his axed-staff in one arm and the other twirled my wig's curls.

"Well, I want a turn with this one. She reminds me of a girl I used to know. I like a woman with strong features." The Guard said and actually started kissing Shortblade's hand as he put his staff against the wall.

"I guess you can have a go first but then I want a turn. I can keep busy with this smaller one. Her buxom breasts are perfect." The other Guard said and laughed as he drank from a flask he pulled out from under his tunic.

"Perfect for what?" The Guard said as he laughed.

"Holding my posset and my hands." The other Guard said as he unlocked the gate for us and started walking down the stairs to the dungeons.

The other Guard stopped and unlocked a second door once we got to the bottom floor. Shortblade and I followed them down giggling; with our long gowns flowing mischievously. And both Guard's eyes and smiles couldn't stop looking back at Shortblade.

My corset was very loose and bulky with the added weapons under my crinoline. *Thank the sea they fancy Shortblade or else they'd feel the dagger before I plunge. My picking-keys are barely hidden under my breasts; we just need to get closer to the cells.* I thought as I saw the long hallway of bars but both Guards stopped and now like vultures went to Shortblade. The one Guard was trying to undue Shortblade's corset and the other had grabbed Shortblade's hand.

"Here my strong wench. This is what you need right here." The other Guard said as he placed Shortblade's hand under the russet of his tunic and started kissing him aggressively.

My eyes widened as Shortblade started kissing him back with a sizzling urge of his moving hands. And they all completely ignored me pulling out a dagger. I went up behind the Guard whose hands were flipping Shortblade's skirts and as the Guard gasped in his rather large discovery; I slit his throat. The other Guard was locked in a heated kiss as he suddenly groaned and fell to the ground beside a ripped off loin cloth. Shortblade had pulled the Guard's own dagger and plunged it vengeful into his chest.

"Shortblade, you tawdry temptress. I thought you were going to rip his vanquished pants right off." I said and laughed as I grabbed the long metal keys.

"Well he be' a lusty, mawkish pantler and much too common for my distinction." Shortblade said as he bent over out of breath and grabbed his loin cloth from the dirt floor.

After carefully re-attaching the long leather; he pulled down his skirts. One dangerous weapon was much larger than Luna's laughter deserved under his newly secure loincloth and I cleared my throat loudly turning away as he caught my eyes with a charmed smile.

"What was with the kisses and hands Shortblade?" I said still a little shocked by his boldness.

"I had to convince them we were up for a celebration or they wouldn't have let us in." Shortblade said out of breath.

"I think they would have let us in just to taste your beauty." I said.

"Oh you make me blush but the color of this dress really does nothing for my gorgeous skin tone." He said and winked while I rolled my eyes.

We quickly ran down the long stone hallway and came upon the holds where they were being kept. The crew didn't even look as we stood before them. It was as if they had their free spirit beat out of them and were half the men I knew and loved.

The sight was unnerving as the Pirate King lay chained with six heavy locks attached and plunged daggers wrapped in the twisted chains bound to his unmoving body. A heavy silver cross lay scorching the Pirate King's forehead in a locked chain and looked like it was burning in a blue flame against his head.

"Oh Captain." I cried out as I struggled in trying to find the right key to unlock the caged door.

"Dragonfly you came. What are you and Shortblade doing dressed as ladies?" Hatley said disheartened.

"We have come to rescue you." I said as I fiddled with the Guard's keys and clicked to open the metal door with a creak.

Then I felt the sharp tip to my back and I turned to face the weapon piercing me; only to be struck hard across my face.

❦❦❦

CHAPTER 25

I touched my shoulder feeling the warm liquid flowing and looked at my hand covered in crimson fluid. I squinted with my good eye that looked over to a bloody Shortblade in his long undergarments and I gasped as I looked down and saw that I was in my long chemise as well. Our fancy dresses, my wig, corsets, stockings, boots and weapons were all gone. I looked up and seen O'Shady smiling wickedly at Shortblade.

"O'Shady? What have you done? A pox on you for selling us out." I said as I spit blood on the dirty stone floor and wearily sat up with Shortblade's help.

"I hoped you were dead. Because I knew you and Shortblade would try rescuing them. As soon as I saw your arrows in those guards' heads, I knew it was you. Dragonfly you are a skilled marksman but I suspected something odd about you. And I was right. You be' a charlatan all this time. You are too repulsive for thine eyes to gaze upon. King

Vermin shall hang ye finely with everyone else. I offered your unconscious body to my knights and your filth was too repugnant for them. Ye shall die here in disgrace just like everyone else. While your toes lift Dragonfly, I shall be drinking my nice posset in my glorious castle. It's a shame really, all that talent wasted on a woman." O'Shady said and laughed at our misery.

"Dragonfly we were sold out by this scoundrel and Madeira to the Evil King Vermin. I had thought you were killed with the ladies." Hatley said as he gulped.

I looked over at Hatley's deep frown. My face was similar and it held no tears over our situation. In a thousand years I would still choose being a pirate over being an arsehole.

O'Shady looked malicious at my light chemise undergarment and I shivered at his ill intent. Without words Shortblade took off his chemise and passed it to me to cover my see through cotton. I quickly placed it over my own under garment and mouthed the word thanks as he nodded.

"Shortblade that leather loincloth is very unladylike. Me, I prefer the slit-crotch pantaloons. Just like the ones Madeira wore when she tried to save herself by seducing me. Although, I'm not as endowed as you or your Monster King; I was gifted more brains than you both. And I hung her in the square already to give the crowd a nice show." O'Shady said and laughed like a maniac in the despaired emptiness of the dungeon.

"Okay I have to run; my castle waits just off the eastside of Trenton in the countryside by the sea. Tis' a glorious thing that ye all shall never see unless ye join me. Any men willing to serve me can come now or rot here before your neck gets snapped." O'Shady said as he held the barred door open and some men stood up.

"What? Our men are loyal and only follow the Pirate King's lead not some impotent little sea urchin." Hatley shouted.

"Careful Hatley, I like you. But even that butterfly has abandoned your sinking ship. If I really cared, I'd do ye through right now. So much for the Great Pirate King of Hell. He was nobody, just like all of ye." O'Shady shouted as he looked at me and spit on the ground.

"And won't anyone address Dragonfly's deception. I may be a villain but open your eyes. You have all been deceived by this wench. Dragonfly is a woman of all things. She should hang with Madeira for that treachery, just like the vile she is." O'Shady shouted and laughed like the fool he was.

O'Shady moved closer to strike me but Shortblade moved in front of me taking the brunt of the blow. I was furious and I hoped my good eye burned a hole in his head with my hatred I didn't hide.

"Why are you doing this?" I said in distaste.

"Because with all of you captured and the final death of the Great Sun Dancer King; I can go back to high society. I can finally have my own castle and land back from King Vermin; which was confiscated out of unpaid taxes." O'Shady sneered.

"All of this was to get back your castle? To what of honor and freedom will your soul have left?" Shortblade said.

"I would rather be rich from my owed inheritance; not from some booty." O'Shady said cool as he clanged the heavy door shut leaving us to our sadistic fate.

"Ye' shall be rich in cowardice. Your gold shall bury your grave ye' dig." I shouted but he ignored me.

I listened to each metal-barred door chime shut in a terrifying echo like the bells of some cathedral of the damned. Next I could hear cannons and guns go off from the courtyard.

There were in total five heartless men who had saved their necks by walking out of the cell. They hadn't served under the Pirate King long and hadn't taken the oath or test. When O'Shady left he took them; our weapons; both sets of my picking-keys; and our dresses just to be a cad.

I looked over to the men and sat against the wall as we listened to drums from the courtyard and a flute playing like it was a festive occasion. Every now and then I could hear loud cannons booming in the background.

Shortblade sat beside me and his face looked like mine felt. I could only use my left eye, the other was so sore and my right shoulder had a deep puncture like a knife had went in me where blood slowly trickled out.

Suddenly the window high in the cell streamed sunshine across the floor and I placed my hand out to feel the light. When I looked at Shortblade his sadness overwhelmed me. But as he looked down something glinted in his scuffled curled tresses. I placed my hand on his bruised cheek and then through his hair without speaking. He faintly smiled as I pulled out two hair pins that had been still holding his golden curls. I smiled weakly at him and he winked as I walked over to the Pirate King's motionless body.

The Pirate King's face was shaved and his long black hair was chopped off with even shorter patches where the hair was cut or ripped from his bloody scalp. His left eye had a massive slice down the center and it looked as if they had tried to steal it from his head unsuccessfully. Even his golden earring had been almost ripped from his torn earlobe and dangled in a red dried puddle.

"Dragonfly it is silver; all of it. The bastards knew his only weakness and they tortured him for pleasure." Hatley said as he looked away quickly.

My hand caressed Dragon's noble face that was clearly beaten, just like his body. My tears silently fell as I looked at his brutal peace. The Evil King Vermin of Bristol had stripped Dragon of everything, even his dignity as he lay there with silver chains around his broken body. Everywhere the silver touched was smoking as it burned his rotting flesh.

Even all six silver daggers locked deep inside him were leaving fried holes to his internal organs.

My arms were more than sore. They were weak as I lifted it to pick the lock on Dragon's forehead that was holding the excessive silver cross. With the first click I quickly moved the cross away and it revealed his red skull and a black rotting brain which the metal had burned into.

My tears stung my face as I looked on at the horrors they had done to him and I worked faster carefully freeing each lock and then took out each deep dagger. I could feel the men's eyes on me but I kept going at freeing my King. With each click I felt hope in my soul stir. Removing the last daggers that were in Dragon's heart and stomach were a little trickier. As I removed the blade from his heart I gasped seeing the sharp tip through our wedding ring plunged deep inside his heart burning a black hole. Then I removed the dagger through his bowels and intestines. I exhaled loudly as I moved the heavy silver chains and Shortblade got up to help me pull them the rest of the way off. The heavy chains smoked in burning the Pirate King's blue flesh as each came off.

Removing the chains revealed how they had gutted him from his belly button downwards exposing his rotting intestines that had been pulled out. As our silent tears fell we tried to carefully place Dragon's intestines back in. Together we moved all the cruel silver items away from Dragon and into the furthest corner of the cell. I took off the extra chemise that Shortblade had given me and covered Dragon as best as I could while kissing his cheek.

"Dragonfly he is gone. I wanted to save him too, but he has been long dead in trying to save the ladies from the tree's trap. That was how they captured him." Hatley bitterly said but no more than finished his sentence and the Pirate King sat up.

All of the men jumped and gasped including Shortblade. But I looked over to Dragon and smiled as my tears came down.

"Dragonfly come here." His deep scruffy voice said as I willingly came to his side and his glowing red eyes scanned me.

"You have freed me. But I see our secrets have been revealed. I need blood to heal my love." His voice was dark and inhuman as he spoke to me.

His arms were outreached to me and his fangs were elongating as I moved even closer to him.

"Take what's left of my strength and free us my King." I said as he gently took my hand and kissed it.

"Aye Captain. I donate my blood for your strength." Hatley shouted and bowed.

"I shall give my blood for your strength. Long live the Great Pirate King." Shortblade said and bowed immediately.

"Aye Aye. For the love of our Great Pirate King." The men all cheered and bowed their heads as they lined up.

"I am weak from the silver. I will need much blood to heal myself and seek vengeance on all that have deceived us." The Pirate King said as his voice became rich in lower octaves.

I heard a few men gasp as he instantly morphed to the monster I am madly in love with. He is actually a pale blue and resembled a mammoth leathery humanoid-bat like creature. His once soft feathered wings took on sinister textures resembling sandpaper and beat leather. The only thing that resembled the man that a moment before stood was his short black hair and the golden earring in his giant long ears. His great wings spread out and he let out a ferocious roar through the dungeon. As he held his arms still out for me and saw my bare neck; he roared with a deeper rage. But tenderly took me in his arms.

I watched as his long clawed hands hovered over my wounded shoulder. With his eyes closed, his hand glowed as it paused over my wound and healed it. He took his wedding ring and placed it in my hand while he finished ripping the golden ring from his earlobe. He placed the other ring in my palm too and said some ancient words as a green mist spread around the rings transforming them to matching wedding bands. With his large monster claws he carefully slipped one on my left finger as he placed the other on his left finger. Then he kissed my neck and sank his teeth in, as I gasped.

The men stood still in knowing our King gave mercy in people that showed fearless valor. As he drank from me his wings started changing from the leathery sludge to feathery forms. My quivering body was out of oxygen as I felt his hot breath on my neck and then his sensual kiss. As his warm breath spread across me, I felt a loving healing energy all over.

With each crew member who gladly gave their neck; the Pirate King started looking more human-like and his feathers became softer like fluffy clouds. He drank from and healed each member of our real pirate clan. And we all stood in awe at our healed Pirate King who now resembled a beautiful Angel of Darkness than the ferocious human we knew him to be or the pale blue vampiric monster that he was before.

"Hatley acquire the sister ship of Telulahs Revenge. And let us be free of here. Bristol is going to bath in all the fires of hell I bring and the coble streets will flow with the river of blood from our enemies." Dragon's voice was so dark it sent a chill in the air and I saw my breath.

Then his whole body glowed while his great wings retracted into his back and he screamed painfully into a howl. His sun-kissed flesh ripped from his body transforming him into an enormous black-furred demon-werewolf. His menacing razor-like fangs and six inch claws were a fearsome sight but we cheered him on. He howled long in a gruesome tone of a murderous revenge.

He smashed through the bars like they were flower petals and we tried to follow his pure rage. But he charged forward like a menacing hurricane, unstoppable in the swift blood vengeance he brought and we could hear the unrelenting screams on the streets.

As we made our way out of the jail he was gone but the gore and carnage was left. The Hell Hound of Legends would have his day in the high sun. No mercy would be given to the enemy; just like the ruthless acts they had spared us pirates and our fellow hanging comrades.

My heart didn't hold any remorse for the Royal Guards I passed that had their necks torn through. I smiled and associated their deaths due to their plague of actions over the years of anguish; even inflicted on me in my youth. My hero was rampaging and making the streets a sweet crimson color that matched my emotions of revenge.

My truly Great Pirate King had left an awe of desolation and I felt that rage within his soul. I wished to join him in his feast on the blood of our enemies. But my weak mortal heart was not meant for his bringer of demise.

We continued through the ravished streets hearing the gruesome howling as we walked through the blood-stained roads. We watched as other pirate clans had rushed through the streets to come to our aide and burned the gallows down. Bristol was bathing in blood and I knew the carnage would carry to the meaningless castles and countryside's of Trenton as our King harvested vengeance on all who had wronged us. Even the brave knights crumpled at the sight of the werewolf that ripped them apart without effort.

As the Great Pirate King eradicated our enemies, a horrific fire spread through the lands. The flames were so high they burned in my soul matching the deep wounds in my heart from the people I loved who weren't able to rise from the grave. My heart wept over the only beheaded mother I ever knew.

CHAPTER 26

I drearily paused down an alley seeing my fine dress that was stolen just peeking out the corner of my eye. Its fine silk was tattered and bloody as I slipped it on. My ego had been decapitated and I didn't have any super-powers of darkness to fall back on. I was deeply injured at being just an ordinary girl again. I was just a stupid woman in a powerful man's world. I wondered what would become of me as I headed to the only place I could think of.

Alone I made my way to the sandy beach where our small row boats had been kept and tried to remain hopeful as I dragged my feet. With my bloody wig in my hands and my dress a bloody fray; I moved forward with my eyes down.

I glanced up and saw first mate Hatley. His feathered hat was covered with ash as well as his heavy buckled coat. It looked ravished like he had salvaged it from the ruble of the smoldering tavern. He had this menacing look about his face as he tapped his giant buckled boot impatiently on the dock.

And out on the thick black-smoked horizon of calming blue; our new Telulahs Revenge gently rocked beside the other little row boats. I could see all the busy bodies boarding and getting ready for departure. And I stopped three feet shy of the hug I wanted desperately from my friend and the only father figure I had ever known.

"Well..." Hatley's voice growled and I saw two other familiar crewmates with him frowning as they looked at me.

Shortblade and Sully stood with their arms crossed by Hatley's side as his brows crinkled and he continued to tap his foot almost in a stomp.

"I'm so sorry Hatley. I wanted to tell you...I..." I beseeched to his heart.

"Well enough already. You've made us wait for your petticoat while the sun is fading in the afternoon's light. Get your arse on the boat already so we can go home. We all need to take position." Hatley said and gave me the biggest bear hug ever as I heard my bones crack.

"Yes, Sir. Wait, we need to wait for the Captain." I shouted as we were already in the water and rowing towards the ship.

"He's coming. Dragonfly, you little fairy rascal. You will take lookout in the nest like always. But you'll have to change; we can't have you looking prettier than the Captain." Hatley said and winked at my astonished grin.

Shortblade and Sully had huge grins for me as they rowed.

"Besides we all know Shortblade is too pretty for his own good." Sully said and jabbed Shortblade in the ribs in play.

"You're just jealous, I know this. I can't help it if I was born from beauty's breast." Shortblade said and laughed.

I looked at Sully and noticed a lace ribbon fall out of his pocket onto Shortblade's loin clothed lap and he quickly grabbed it. He hid it back into his pocket but winked at me and I gave him a warm smile.

Then we both smiled looking at Shortblade and I watched his muscles glistening in the golden sun. Shortblade really was dazzling. He hadn't bothered to find any clothes and rowed quite happily with his loin cloth dangling. *Jeeze, Shortblade do you have to show off your magnificence to everyone?* I thought as I turned away from his radiance.

"There she be' the new Telulahs Revenge. Tis' a perfect ship, just like the last sixteen Telulahs Revenge we've had." Hatley chuckled.

"There have been sixteen Telulahs Revenge ships before this? Do you think maybe the name should be changed?" Shortblade heckled Hatley.

Hatley scratched his chin and smoothed down his long red beard. He looked to be in great thought and then cleared his throat.

"I reckon it may be time." Hatley said and belly laughed so hearty a button popped off his shirt and we joined in laughter.

We were the last crewmates to board our new Telulahs Revenge and as I climbed onto the deck everyone teased and greeted me the same. I went down to the room that awaited me with extra fabric, shirt, vest and pants. I was grateful for my old clothes and black bandana to cover up my curly red hair. *I can't believe it. They know I'm a girl and still I belong. I'm already being teased about my breakfast sausage, but even that is great. These men are my family and even through losing everything; the part left is real. We all have each other's backs. And our Captain has our hearts and souls; along with Telulahs Revenge.* I thought as I dressed quickly.

When I came back in a flash I was just going to climb the mast when I heard; "Captain Ahoy" from Sully.

Just then a dark shadow flew and touched down on the deck. Everyone toed the line immediately as the Great Pirate King transformed to the vicious man we all knew and all loved. He turned quickly to change into the waiting clothes and then inspected his remaining crew as we held our breath sticking our chests out in attention. Without saying a word his red eyes scanned us all. And as his sharp eyes were inspecting us I stood at attention but looked at the fires burning on the shore and the castles that were crumbling. The black smoke filled the red flames of the sun setting on the Evil King of Bristol's fiery end.

"Today was a sad day men and although our enemy has been vanquished; the sadness lingers for those we lost. Take special care as we travel and rest if need be. Dragonfly I will need a tea to drown out the muddy blood of the Bristol Kingdom I just ingested." The Pirate King's voice seemed ominous and still octaves lower than his normal scruff of a voice.

"Yes Sir." I said but stilled as he continued.

"There will always be enemies, my fearless pirate clan but if your loyalty stays true your black sails will always fly higher with me." The Pirate King's deep voice had a rough edge to it and I watched my cold breath in the air.

"Hatley as I was flying I found this little one alone in the burning blacksmith's hut. I think we should call him *'Cut-Throat Trenton'* in honor of our fallen Kathleen." The Pirate King said as he pulled out the little fluffy black kitten from his inside coat pocket and handed him to Hatley's waiting open arms.

"I also noticed our ships name was written; *'Telulahs Revenge II'*. I think the new name is fitting." The Pirate King said in a husky voice and smiled.

"Thank you Captain, I thought it was time." Hatley said as he beamed.

Hatley stuck out his chest with a grin as I looked over to Shortblade who seemed to sigh as he rolled his eyes and then became a giant mush as Hatley passed him the small kitten.

"Hatley take the helm we are headed to Medusa's Pyramid down past the southern point of the equator. It is an untraveled area where there are tales of monsters far greater than I. But the treasure is far greater as well. Continue on our course with the night crew. Everyone dismissed." The Captain bellowed as he made his way to his quarters.

I hurried to the galley and made him a special tea. I went down past my door to his and knocked gently.

"Dragonfly, you never have to knock again. Every being of me is here because you freed me. I am at your loving mercy." His deep voice whispered to my soul as he bowed to me and then took me in his arms; placing sweet kisses all over me.

Before I knew it we were wrapped in sheets and divine ecstasy as his wings emerged out of his back. With his climax his wings opened and he covered me with his feathers and heavy breath. His skin had turned a light pale blue and he suddenly flew over to the window turning from me in the afternoon sun.

I slowly walked over to him and gently placed my hands to his scar-filled back. His soft black feathers were darker than a raven's but softer than the down on a chick and hung down the whole length of his frame. He had his huge clawed hands covering his face. My hands reached his and pulled them slowly down.

"Please my Queen. I have never wished to frighten you." The darkness in his voice was undeniable.

"Dragon I hold a secret in my heart. I know your light and I know your darkness. And I am still here." I whispered as I moved his hand and kissed it placing it over my heart.

His body was slightly turned from me and with my other hand I turned him to face me. My hand held his rough clawed hand over my heart and my other hand caressed his long bat ears moving down to the side of his chiseled jaw. His defined cheek bones held a blush as his eyes stayed closed while he exhaled slower revealing his larger fangs.

"This is my true form. I am a monster and a pure creature of darkness." His voice said six octaves lower than his human voice but held softness.

"You are more beautiful than the ocean's blue on a summer's day." I said as I caressed his lovely blue skin.

I gingerly kissed his cheeks and then his blood red lips. His eyes fluttered open and I looked at his larger, glowing-crimson wolf-like eyes. He was too miraculous for words. And I kissed him deep and true of all the love in my soul. He stepped back from my loving embrace and looked to the floor. His monstrous feet wiggled his blue clawed toes.

"How can you be with me knowing my hideousness. Because of how much blood I drank today; it will be a longtime for my human form to stay more permanent. That is why I had to rest and hideaway. It is not in my heart to scare the crew as my true form. Our bond is forever, but I relinquish you from your oath if I am too frightening to be around. I have lived centuries almost completely absent from a woman's warmth; I can do it again." He said in utter sadness and it made a tear escape my eye.

I moved my hand over to his strong bicep and turned him back to me. Gently, I moved his face up to mine and his hand back to my wild beating heart. I smiled sweetly looking into his lovely red eyes.

"I am here because I am completely in love with you Dragon. You have had my heart from the first moment you rescued me. Your undead heart has more feeling and kindness than I have ever known. I can't stop looking at how magnificent and beautiful your graceful soul is. And I reject your counter offer. I never make a promise I don't intend to keep and I promise to love you until the wells of blood are dried up in these veins and there are no oceans to sail anymore. I promised you forever and I expect nothing less." I said and kissed him fierce taking his claw and dragged it over my breast drawing blood.

"My Queen, I promise to love you till all the stars in the sky burn and the Milky Way is but stardust." He said as he kissed me vigorously and then drank from my robust cleavage.

Lovingly he flew us to his bedroom throne of lovely cotton sheets. When he kissed me his dark magic swirled around us and the tingly sensations swept my body as goosebumps. I could feel the power and safety of his arms around me. I was addicted to this euphoric feeling of tranquility with his fierce heart that beat now against my back and he held me tight in lovely rhythm of an enchanted thunder deep inside that enraptured me with his exploding wildfire of passion.

I stayed in his arms until he fell asleep. I comforted his sorrows but he always made me feel like I was more. Softly I kissed his pale blue hand admiring our wedding rings and five-pointed star matching tattoo on our left palms.

He made me feel like I was surrounded in a meadow of wildflowers and sunshine; and that I was eternally safe. I lingered in his loving arms before getting dressed for my crow's nest duty. The ship held our hearts and I needed to join my crew and he needed rest. *I love him so much. Thank you kind Universe for bringing me my hero and husband.* I thought as I looked at him so captivating in the sunlight and covered him up snugly.

He needed me but I knew I had an insatiable need for him. I couldn't escape my desire for his love any less than my lungs needed oxygen to breathe.

CHAPTER 27

It was a peaceful evening all night with calm seas and gentle breezes that moved our sails steady. All the stars lit up the sky for us as we continued on our way. The nest was high up on the main mast and I loved watching the cosmos of streaking and twinkling stars. This night of our freedom was surreal as even Telulah the sea monster was moving slower than ever and not even visible on our horizon, in her silent stalking. She would never stop and one day I just knew it would come to a great battle where lives would be lost but total freedom would be found.

I turned my thoughts and my head to the rising sun in the east seeing the pinkish-purples that I never grew tired of as I watched the vibrant colors of the calm water. I slowly made my descent down the mast as another crewmate was going to start climbing but Hatley came forth on the deck.

"Before the complete shift change all hands on deck the Captain has a message." Hatley yelled down below and repeated himself on deck.

As everyone toed the line, we waited in attention for our King to speak as he made his way from our quarters looking dashing. He had spared not even the smallest attention to detail as his feather stood out through his black hat and his shirt was of the finest quality covered by his coat. He wore his dagger at his sturdy hips and his magnificent eyes were the deep red from the blood; but dazzled in the rays of sunlight. He always took my breath away in his regalness and I looked down in a blush as he winked at me.

"Recent events have shown me our vulnerabilities. You know what I am. Possibly not exactly what I am, but you know I was born a creature of darkness. How am I able to walk in the sun? Evolution my dear family. And now I ask you to be more. I ask you to be brave and trust that what I am offering you is only the greatest opportunity of your lives. Even much greater than the treasure we are traveling to." His deep voice boomed over us and he cleared his throat as he walked back and forth.

"I want you to feast your eyes on this." He said as he pulled out a twisted golden goblet from his long black coat pocket.

The goblet shined in the sun with its golden clawed feet on the base and scribed wings and fins on each side of the cup.

"This empty royal cup is the very cup that changed my life forever in the year 1414 A.D. Yes, I am over three hundred years old and silver is the only thing that can hinder me, but I am immortal. As you can see it is empty. My former lover drank every last bit of Hades blood. But his blood is in my undead veins." His scruffy voice said so dark some of the men held there gasps for a moment and exhaled loudly.

He placed the golden goblet on the compass table where we all could admire its bewitching charm. Then he took a golden jewel encrusted dagger out from his sash and belt around his waist. He held it up to the sun holding the glittering gold band. But when he touched the blade to his right hand his skin started to burn and smoke; as his glowing eyes became a deeper crimson.

"Tis only silver that can hinder me but it will not kill me, as I am undead." He said as he sliced his right hand with the silver blade letting the cup fill with his dark blood to the brim.

He waved his wounded hand and he was magically healed. Then he held the filled cup high for everyone to see.

"I am giving you a choice. Do not feel pressured because you are my familia and it is your free will that I want you to exert without prejudice. I am offering you all a chance at immortality. I am gifting this because you have stood by me these years, even in the face of many dangers. You all have risked your lives and I wish to grant you immortality. If you chose to accept my gift you will be bound by me for all eternity and bound to the thirst for blood each month on the night of the full moon. But you will always have home and family. What say thee my beloved pirates exalted above all the others?" He said in his eerie creature voice so dark but we all knew he spoke only a noble truth.

I immediately stepped forward and he gracefully walked over to me as the golden cup shimmered in a come hither to my heart. I smiled at him and he smiled warmly to me. It was as if his heart leapt in his eyes at me stepping forward. This was my chosen destiny and I couldn't wait for eternity to begin. Bravely, I looked upon the cup of my hopes and dreams with the mysterious crimson fluid that swirled with raw magic. The fluid changed to a bright shimmering yellow before my eyes and resembled liquid gold.

"The future holds the greatest adventure of your lives in acceptance." The Pirate King's deep voice cooed to me and I was hypnotized with my blushing love.

"But what my dear King shall becometh of us?" Shortblade stepped forth along with Sully and the rest of the men.

"Drink and we shall all find out, shan't we?" The Great Pirate King's voice was as smooth as velvet in passing me the cherished cup.

I closed my eyes facing the eastern sunrise and lifted the precious metal to my lips drinking heartily. I could taste lavender and the refreshing loving blood that seemed to penetrate my soul quietly. I could feel the power in my evolution through my veins. My adoring heart sped up and my whimsical thoughts of a cherished forever with my love.

I lingered in my affectionate look into the Pirate King's blood red eyes as his fanged smile grew and he winked. Without taking my eyes off him I passed the cup to Shortblade and heard his gulping of the sweet liquid dreams.

Suddenly, I lay down to the deck and my flickering eyes shut but I felt Shortblade lay beside me as my heart slowly perished.

When my eyes fluttered in waking I felt an uncontrollable, ethereal scream of a howl escape my throat.

♠The End Perhaps…♠

ACKNOWLEDGMENTS

I would really like to express my sincere gratitude to; The Universe, my fans, family, and friends. Its fine people like you that give struggling authors a chance. Thank you again!

I would also like to thank my mechanics and my friends Eric Heldman and Jay Flowers at Cormier's Good Year Obsentia, in Quinte West, Ontario. Thank you for always being great friends and taking care of my car. I am so appreciative that you are lights in the world and practice random acts of kindness every day. Thank you again for not suing me for killing off your characters in future novels! Their website is here if you want some kind individuals helping you with your auto needs and are in the Quinte West Area: https://www.trentontire.ca/

Thank you for reading!   I really hope you have liked my book. Please add a short review and let me know what you thought!

And always let your light shine bright!

A.L. Secord is a pen name for the author APRIL SECORD. She enjoys many genres. But she is most passionate about Dark Fantasy Romance. She loves learning new things, and occasionally burning food for the ones she loves. She is an author, a proud mother, and an avid adventurer of the unknown; on her many pursuits for greater happiness and Bigfoot.

THE HOUSE WINS

A.L. SECORD

FOREST LOVE

BROKEN VAMPIRE PRINCE

A.L. SECORD

THE LAST KING

EVIL TASTES GOOD

A.L. SECORD

<u>**Books by A.L. SECORD**</u>: